William Dean Howells

A Counterfeit Presentment.

Comedy

William Dean Howells

A Counterfeit Presentment.
Comedy

ISBN/EAN: 9783744767439

Printed in Europe, USA, Canada, Australia, Japan

Cover: Foto ©Andreas Hilbeck / pixelio.de

More available books at **www.hansebooks.com**

A Counterfeit Presentment.

COMEDY.

BY

W. D. HOWELLS.

BOSTON:
JAMES R. OSGOOD AND COMPANY.
Late Ticknor & Fields, and Fields, Osgood, & Co.
1877.

RIVERSIDE, CAMBRIDGE:

STEREOTYPED AND PRINTED BY

H. O. HOUGHTON AND COMPANY.

CONTENTS.

I.

AN EXTRAORDINARY RESEMBLANCE.

A COUNTERFEIT PRESENTMENT.

(The Scene is always in the Parlor of the Ponkwasset Hotel.)

———◆———

I.

BARTLETT *and* CUMMINGS.

On a lovely day in September, at that season when the most sentimental of the young maples have begun to redden along the hidden courses of the meadow streams, and the elms, with a sudden impression of despair in their languor, betray flecks of yellow on the green of their pendulous boughs, — on such a day at noon, two young men enter the parlor of the Ponkwasset Hotel, and deposit about the legs of the piano the burdens they have been carrying: a camp-stool, namely, a field-easel, a closed box of colors, and a canvas to which, ap-

parently, some portion of reluctant nature has just
been transferred. These properties belong to one
of the young men, whose general look and bearing
readily identify him as their owner: he has a quick,
somewhat furtive eye, a full brown beard, and hair
that falls in a careless mass down his forehead,
which as he dries it with his handkerchief, sweep-
ing the hair aside, shows broad and white; his
figure is firm and square, without heaviness, and in
his movement as well as in his face there is something of stubbornness, with a suggestion of arro-
gance. The other, who has evidently borne his
share of the common burdens from a sense of good
comradeship, has nothing of the painter in him,
nor anything of this painter's peculiar temper-
ament: he has a very abstracted look and a dark,
dreaming eye; he is pale, and does not look strong.
The painter flings himself into a rocking-chair and
draws a long breath.

Cummings (for that is the name of the slighter
man, who remains standing as he speaks): "It's
warm, is n't it?" His gentle face evinces a curious and kindly interest in his friend's sturdy dem-
onstrations of fatigue.

Bartlett: "Yes, hot — confoundedly." He rubs his handkerchief vigorously across his forehead, and then looks down at his dusty shoes, with apparently no mind to molest them in their dustiness. "The idea of people going back to town in this weather! However, I'm glad they're such asses; it gives me free scope here. Every time I don't hear some young woman banging on that piano, I fall into transports of joy."

Cummings, smiling: "And after to-day you won't be bothered even with me."

Bartlett: "Oh, I shall rather miss you, you know. I like somebody to contradict."

Cummings: "You can contradict the ostler."

Bartlett: "No, I can't. They've sent him away; and I believe you're going to carry off the last of the table-girls with you in the stage to-morrow. The landlord and his wife are to run the concern themselves the rest of the fall. Poor old fellow! The hard times have made lean pickings for him this year. His house wasn't full in the height of the season, and it's been pretty empty since."

Cummings : " I wonder he does n't shut up altogether."

Bartlett : " Well, there are a good many transients, as they call them, at this time of year, — fellows who drive over from the little hill-towns with their girls in buggies, and take dinner and supper; then there are picnics from the larger places, ten and twelve miles off, that come to the grounds on the pond, and he always gets something out of them. And as long as he can hope for anything else, my eight dollars a week are worth hanging on to. Yes, I think I shall stay here all through October. I 've got no orders, and it 's cheap. Besides, I 've managed to get on confidential terms with the local scenery ; I thought we should like each other last summer, and I feel now that we 're ready to swear eternal friendship. I shall do some fairish work here, yet. Phew !" He mops his forehead again, and springing out of his chair he goes up to the canvas, which he has faced to the wall, and turning it about retires some paces, and with a swift, worried glance at the windows falls to considering it critically.

Cummings : "You 've done some fairish work already, if I 'm any judge." He comes to his friend's side, as if to get his effect of the picture. "I don't believe the spirit of a graceful elm that just begins to feel the approach of autumn was ever better interpreted. There is something tremendously tragical to me in the thing. It makes me think of some lovely and charming girl, all grace and tenderness, who finds the first gray hair in her head. I should call that picture The First Gray Hair."

Bartlett, with unheeding petulance : "The whole thing 's too infernally brown ! — I beg your pardon, Cummings : what were you saying ? Go on ! I like your prattle about pictures ; I do, indeed. I like to see how far you art-cultured fellows can miss all that was in a poor devil's mind when he was at work. But I 'd rather you 'd sentimentalize my pictures than moralize them. If there 's anything that makes me quite limp, it 's to have an allegory discovered in one of my poor stupid old landscapes. But The First Gray Hair is n't bad, really. And a good, senseless, sloppy name like that often sells a picture."

Cummings: " You 're brutal, Bartlett. I don't believe your pictures would own you, if they had their way about it."

Bartlett: " And I would n't own *them* if I had *mine.* I 've got about forty that I wish somebody else owned — and I had the money for them; but we seem inseparable. Glad you 're going to-morrow? You *are* a good fellow, Cummings, and I *am* a brute. Come, I 'll make a great concession to friendship: it struck me, too, while I was at work on that elm, that it was something like — an old girl!" Bartlett laughs, and catching his friend by either shoulder twists him about in his strong clutch, while he looks him merrily in the face. " I 'm not a poet, old fellow; and sometimes I think I ought to have been a painter and glazier instead of a mere painter. I believe it would have paid better."

Cummings: " Bartlett, I hate to have you talk in that way."

Bartlett: " Oh, I know it 's a stale kind."

Cummings: " It 's worse than stale. It 's destructive. A man can soon talk himself out of heart with his better self. You can end by really being as sordid-minded and hopeless and low-purposed as you pretend to be. It's insanity."

Bartlett: "Good! I've had my little knock on the head, you know. I don't deny being cracked. But I've a method in my madness."

Cummings: "They all have. But it's a very poor method; and I don't believe you could say just what yours is. You think because a girl on whom you set your fancy — it's nonsense to pretend it was your heart — found out she didn't like you as well as she thought, and honestly told you so in good time, that your wisest course is to take up that rôle of misanthrope which begins with yourself and leaves people to imagine how low an opinion you have of the rest of mankind."

Bartlett: "My dear fellow, you know I always speak well of that young lady. I've invariably told you that she behaved in the handsomest manner. She even expressed the wish — I distinctly remember being struck by the novelty of the wish at the time — that we should remain friends. You misconceive" —

Cummings : "How many poor girls have been jilted who don't go about doing misanthropy, but mope at home and sorrow and sicken over their wrong in secret, — a wrong that attacks not merely their pride, but their life itself. Take the case I was telling you of: did you ever hear of anything more atrocious? And do you compare this little sting to your vanity with a death-blow like that?"

Bartlett : "It's quite impossible to compute the number of jilted girls who take the line you describe. But if it were within the scope of arithmetic, I don't know that a billion of jilted girls would comfort me or reform me. I never could regard myself in that abstract way — a mere unit on one side or other of the balance. My little personal snub goes on rankling beyond the reach of statistical consolation. But even if there were any edification in the case of the young lady in Paris, she's too far off to be an example for me. Take some jilted girl nearer home, Cummings, if you want me to go round sickening and sorrowing in secret. I don't believe you can find any. Women are much tougher about the pericardium than we give them credit for, my dear fellow, — much. I don't see why it should hurt a woman more than a man to be jilted. We shall never truly philosophize this important matter till we regard women with something of the fine penetration and impartiality with which they regard each other. Look at the stabs they give and take — they would kill men! And the graceful ferocity with which they dispatch any of their number who happens to be down is quite unexampled in natural history. How much do you suppose her lady friends have left of that poor girl whose case wrings your foolish bosom all the way from Paris? I don't believe so much as a boot-button. Why, even your correspondent — a very lively woman, by the way — can't conceal under all her indignation her little satisfaction that so *proud* a girl as Miss What's-her-name should have been jilted. Of course, she does n't say it."

Cummings, hotly: " *No*, she does n't say it, and it 's not to your credit to imagine it."

Bartlett, with a laugh: " Oh, I don't ask any praise for the discovery. You deserve praise for not making it. It does honor to your good heart. Well, don't be vexed, old fellow. And in trying to improve me on this little point — a weak point, I'll allow, with me — do me the justice to remember that I did n't flaunt my misanthropy, as you call it, in your face ; I did n't force my confidence upon you."

Cummings, with compunction : "I did n't mean to hurt your feelings, Bartlett."

Bartlett : "Well, you have n't. It's all right."

Cummings, with anxious concern : "I wish I could think so."

Bartlett, dryly : "You have *my* leave — my request, in fact." He takes a turn about the room, thrusting his fingers through the hair on his forehead, and letting it fall in a heavy tangle, and then pulling at either side of his parted beard. In facing away from one of the sofas at the end of the room, he looks back over his shoulder at it, falters, wheels about, and picks up from it a lady's shawl and hat. "Hallo!" He lets the shawl fall again into picturesque folds on the sofa. "This is the spoil of no local beauty, Cummings. Look here; I don't understand this. There has been an arrival."

Cummings, joining his friend in contemplation of the hat and shawl: "Yes; it's an arrival beyond all question. Those are a *lady's* things. I should think that was a Paris hat." They remain looking at the things some moments in silence.

Bartlett: "How should a Paris hat get here? I know the landlord was n't expecting it. But it can't be going to stay; it's here through some caprice. It may be a transient of quality, but it's a transient. I suppose we shall see the young woman belonging to it at dinner." He sets the hat on his fist, and holds it at arm's length from him. "What a curious thing it is about clothes"—

Cummings: "Don't, Bartlett, don't!"

Bartlett: "Why?"

Cummings: "I don't know. It makes me feel as if you were offering an indignity to the young lady herself."

Bartlett: "You express my idea exactly. This frippery has not only the girl's personality but her very spirit in it. This hat looks like her; you can infer the whole woman from it, body and soul. It has a conscious air, and so has the shawl, as if they had been eavesdropping and had understood everything we were saying. They know all about my heart-break, and so will she as soon as she puts them on ; she will be interested in me. The hat 's in good taste, is n't it ? "

Cummings, with sensitive reverence for the millinery which his friend handles so daringly : " Exquisite, it seems to me ; but I don't know about such things."

Bartlett : " Neither do I ; but I feel about them. Besides, a painter and glazier sees some things that are hidden from even a progressive minister. Let us interpret the lovely being from her hat. This knot of pale-blue flowers betrays her a blonde ; this lace, this mass of silky, fluffy, cobwebby what-do-you-call-it, and this delicate straw fabric show that she is slight ; a stout woman would kill it, or die in the attempt. And I fancy — here pure inspiration comes to my aid — that she is tallish. I 'm afraid of her ! No — wait ! The shawl has something to say." He takes it up and catches it across his arm, where he scans it critically. "I don't know that I understand the shawl, exactly. It proves her of a good height, — a short woman would n't, or had better not, wear a shawl, — but this black color : should you think it was mourning? Have we a lovely young widow among us?"

Cummings: "I don't see how it could go with the hat, if it were."

Bartlett: "True; the hat is very pensive in tone, but it is n't mourning. This shawl's very light, it's very warm; I construct from it a pretty invalid." He lets the shawl slip down his arm to his hand, and flings it back upon the sofa. "We return from the young lady's heart to her brain — where she carries her sentiments. She has a nice taste in perfumes, Cummings : faintest violet; that goes with the blue. Of what religion is a young lady who uses violet, my reverend friend?"

Cummings: "Bartlett, you 're outrageous. Put down that hat!"

Bartlett: "No, seriously. What is her little æsthetic specialty? Does she sketch? Does she scribble? Tell me, thou wicked hat, does she flirt? Come; out with the vows that you have heard poured into the shelly ear under this knot of pale-blue flowers! Where be her gibes now, her gambols, her flashes of merriment? Now get you to my lady's chamber, and tell her, let her paint an inch thick, to this favor she must come; make her laugh at that. Dost thou think, Horatio Cummings, Cleopatra looked o' this fashion? And smelt so?" — he presses the knot of artificial flowers to his mustache — "Pah!" He tosses the hat on the sofa and walks away.

Cummings: "Bartlett, this is atrocious. I protest" —

Bartlett: "Well, give me up, I tell you." He returns, and takes his friend by the shoulders, as before, and laughs. "I'm not worth your refined pains. I might be good, at a pinch, but I never could be truly lady-like."

Cummings: "You like to speak an infinite deal of nothing, don't you?"

Bartlett: "It's the only thing that makes conversation." As he releases Cummings, and turns

away from him, in the doorway he confronts an
elderly gentleman, whose white hair and white
mustache give distinction to his handsome florid
face. There is something military in his port, as
he stands immovably erect upon the threshold, his
left hand lodged in the breast of his frock-coat, and
his head carried with an officer-like air of command. His visage grows momently redder and
redder, and his blue eyes blaze upon Bartlett with
a fascinated glare that briefly preludes the burst of
fury with which he advances toward him.

II

GENERAL WYATT, BARTLETT, *and* CUMMINGS.

General Wyatt : " You infernal scoundrel ! What are you doing here ? " He raises his stick at Bartlett, who remains motionlessly frowning in wrathful bewilderment, his strong hand knotting itself into a fist where it hangs at his side, while Cummings starts toward them in dismay, with his hand raised to interpose. " Did n't I tell you if I ever set eyes on you again, you villain — did n't I warn you that if you ever crossed my path, you " — He stops with a violent self-arrest, and lets his stick drop as he throws up both his hands in amaze. " Good Heavens ! It 's a mistake ! I beg your pardon, sir ; I do, indeed." He lets fall his hands, and stands staring into Bartlett's face with his illusion apparently not fully dispelled. " A mistake, sir, a mistake. I was misled, sir, by the most prodigious resemblance" — At the sound of voices in the corridor without, he turns from Bartlett, and starts back toward the door.

A Voice, very sweet and weak, without: "I left them in here, I think."

Another Voice: "You must sit down, Constance, and let me look."

The First Voice: "Oh, they'll be here."

General Wyatt, in a loud and anxious tone: "Margaret, Margaret! Don't bring Constance in here! Go away!" At the moment he reaches the door by which he came in, two ladies in black enter the parlor by the other door, the younger leaning weakly on the arm of the elder, and with a languidly drooping head letting her eyes rove listlessly about over the chairs and sofas. With an abrupt start at sight of Bartlett, who has mechanically turned toward them, the elder lady arrests their movement.

III.

MRS. WYATT, CONSTANCE, *and the others.*

Mrs. Wyatt: "Oh, in mercy's name!" The young lady wearily lifts her eyes; they fall upon Bartlett's face, and a low cry parts her lips as she approaches a pace or two nearer, releasing her arm from her mother's.

Constance: "Ah!" She stops; her thin hands waver before her face, as if to clear or to obstruct her vision, and all at once she sinks forward into a little slender heap upon the floor, almost at Bartlett's feet. He instantly drops upon his knees beside her, and stoops over her to lift her up.

Mrs. Wyatt: "Don't touch her, you cruel wretch! Your touch is poison; the sight of you is murder!" Kneeling on the other side of her daughter, she sets both her hands against his breast and pushes him back.

General Wyatt: "Margaret, stop! Look! Look at him again! It is n't *he!*"

Mrs. Wyatt: "Not he? Don't tell me! What?" She clutches Bartlett's arm, and scans his face with dilating eyes. "Oh! it is n't, it is n't! But go away,—go away, all the same! You may be an innocent man, but she would perish in your presence. Keep your hands from her, sir! If your wicked heart is not yet satisfied with your wicked work— Excuse me; I *don't* know what I'm saying! But if you have any pity in your faithless soul —I— oh, *speak* for me, James, and send him —implore him to go away!" She bows her face over her daughter's pale visage, and sobs.

General Wyatt: "Sir, you must pardon us, and have the great goodness to be patient. You have a right to feel yourself aggrieved by what has happened, but no wrong is meant,— no offense. You must be so kind as to go away. I will make you all the needed apologies and explanations." He stoops over his daughter, as Bartlett, in a sort of daze, rises from his knees and retires a few steps. "I beg your pardon, sir," —addressing himself to

Cummings, — "will you help me a moment?" Cummings, with delicate sympathy and tenderness, lifts the arms of the insensible girl to her father's neck, and assists the General to rise with his burden. "Thanks! She's hardly heavier, poor child, than a ghost." The tears stand in his eyes, as he gathers her closer to him and kisses her wan cheek. "Sir," — as he moves away he speaks to Bartlett, — "do me the favor to remain here till I can return to offer you reparation." He makes a stately effort to bow to Bartlett in leaving the room, while his wife, who follows with the young lady's hat and shawl, looks back at the painter with open abhorrence.

IV.

Bartlett *and* Cummings.

Bartlett, turning to his friend from the retreating group on which he has kept his eyes steadfastly fixed: "Where are their keepers?" He is pale with suppressed rage.

Cummings : "Their keepers?"

Bartlett, savagely: "Yes! Have they escaped from them, or is it one of the new ideas to let lunatics go about the country alone? If that old fool hadn't dropped his stick, I'd have knocked him over that table in another instant. And that other old maniac, — what did she mean by pushing me back in that way? How do you account for this thing, Cummings? What do you make of it?"

Cummings : "I don't know, upon my word. There seems to be some mystery, — some painful mystery. But the gentleman will be back directly, I suppose, and "—

Bartlett, crushing his hat over his eyes: "I'll leave you to receive him and his mystery. I've had enough of both." He moves toward the door.

Cummings, detaining him: "Bartlett, you're surely not going away?"

Bartlett: "Yes, I am!"

Cummings: "But he'll be here in a moment. He said he would come back and satisfy the claim which you certainly have to an explanation."

Bartlett, furiously: "Claim? I've a perfect Alabama Claim to an explanation. He can't satisfy it; he shall not try. It's a little too much to expect me to be satisfied with anything he can say after what's passed. Get out of the way, Cummings, or I'll put you on top of the piano."

Cummings: "You may throw me out of the window, if you like, but not till I've done my best to keep you here. It's a shame, it's a crime to go away. You talk about lunatics: you're a raving madman, yourself. Have one glimmer of reason, do; and see what you're about. It's a mistake; it's a misunderstanding. It's his right, it's your duty, to have it cleared up. Come, you've a conscience, Bartlett, and a clean one. Don't give way to your abominable temper. What? You won't stay? Bartlett, I blush for you!"

Bartlett: "Blush unseen, then!" He thrusts Cummings aside and pushes furiously from the room. Cummings looks into the corridor after him, and then returns, panting, to the piano, and mechanically rearranges the things at its feet; he walks nervously away, and takes some turns up and down the room, looking utterly bewildered, and apparently uncertain whether to go or stay. But he has decided upon the only course really open to him by sinking down into one of the arm-chairs, when General Wyatt appears at the threshold of the door on the right of the piano. Cummings rises and comes forward in great embarrassment to meet him.

V

Cummings *and* General Wyatt.

General Wyatt, with a look of surprise at not seeing Bartlett: " The other gentleman "—

Cummings: "My friend has gone out. I hope he will return soon. He has — I hardly know what to say to you, sir. He has done himself great injustice ; but it was natural that under the circumstances " —

General Wyatt, with hurt pride: "Perfectly. I should have lost my temper, too ; but I think I should have waited at the request — the prayer of an older man. I don't mind his temper ; the other villain had *no* temper. Sir, am I right in addressing you as the Rev. Arthur Cummings ? "

Cummings: "My name is Arthur Cummings. I am a minister."

General Wyatt: " I thought I was not mistaken

this time. I heard you preach last Sunday in Boston ; and I know your cousin, Major Cummings of the 34th Artillery. I am General Wyatt."

Cummings, with a start of painful surprise and sympathy : " General Wyatt ? "

General Wyatt, keenly : " Your cousin has mentioned me to you ? "

Cummings : " Yes, — oh yes, certainly ; certainly, very often, General Wyatt. But " — endeavoring to recover himself — " your name is known to us all, and honored. I — I am glad to see you back ; I — understood you were in Paris."

General Wyatt, with fierce defiance : "I was in Paris three weeks ago." Some moments of awkward silence ensue, during which General Wyatt does not relax his angry attitude.

Cummings, finally : "I am sorry my friend is not here to meet you. I ought to say, in justice to him, that his hasty temper does great wrong to his heart and judgment."

General Wyatt : "Why, yes, sir ; so does mine, — so does mine."

Cummings, with a respectful smile lost upon the

General : "And I know that he will certainly be grieved in this instance to have yielded to it."

General Wyatt, with sudden meekness : " I hope so, sir. But I am not altogether sorry that he has done it. I have not only an explanation but a request to make, — a very great and strange favor to ask, — and I am not sure that I should be able to treat him civilly enough throughout an entire interview to ask it properly." Cummings listens with an air of attentive respect, but makes, to this strange statement, no response other than a look of question, while the General pokes about on the carpet at his feet with the point of his stick for a moment before he brings it resolutely down upon the floor with a thump, and resumes, fiercely again : " Sir, your friend is the victim of an extraordinary resemblance, which is so much more painful to us than we could have made it to him that I have to struggle with my reason to believe that the apology should not come from his side rather than mine. He may feel that we have outraged him, but every look of his, every movement, every tone of his voice, is a mortal wound, a deadly insult to us.

He should not live, sir, in the same solar system!"
The General deals the floor another stab with his
cane, while his eyes burn vindictively upon the
mild brown orbs of Cummings, wide open with as-
tonishment. He falters, with returning consciousness of his attitude: "I — I beg your pardon, sir;
I am ridiculous." He closes his lips pathetically,
and lets fall his head. When he lifts it again, it is
to address Cummings with a singular gentleness:
"I know that I speak to a gentleman."

Cummings: "I try to be a good man."

General Wyatt: "I had formed that idea of you,
sir, in the pulpit. Will you do me the great kindness to answer a question, personal to myself, which
I must ask?"

Cummings: "By all means."

General Wyatt: "You spoke of supposing me
still in Paris. Are you aware of any circumstances — painful circumstances — connected with my
presence there? Pardon my asking; I would n't
press you if I could help."

Cummings, with reluctance: "I had just heard
something about — a letter from a friend" —

General Wyatt, bitterly : "The news has traveled fast. Well, sir, a curious chance — a pitiless caprice of destiny — connects your friend with that miserable story." At Cummings's look of amaze : "Through no fault of his, sir ; through no fault of his. Sir, I shall not seem to obtrude my trouble unjustifiably upon you when I tell you how ; you will see that it was necessary for me to speak. I am glad you already know something of the affair, and I am sure that you will regard what I have to say with the right feeling of a gentleman, — of, as you say, a good man."   .

Cummings : "Whatever you think necessary to say to me shall be sacred. But I hope you won't feel that it is necessary to say anything more. I am confident that when my friend has your assurance from me that what has happened is the result of a distressing association " —

General Wyatt : "I thank you, sir. But something more is due to him ; how much more you shall judge. Something more is due to us : I wish to preserve the appearance of sanity, in his eyes and your own. Nevertheless " — the General's tone and bearing perceptibly stiffen — "if you are reluctant" —

Cummings, with reverent cordiality : " General Wyatt, I shall feel deeply honored by whatever confidence you repose in me. I need not say how dear your fame is to us all." General Wyatt, visibly moved, bows to the young minister. " It was only on your account that I hesitated."

General Wyatt: "Thanks. I understand. I will be explicit, but I will try to be brief. Your friend bears this striking, this painful resemblance to the man who has brought this blight upon us all; yes, sir," — at Cummings's look of depreca- tion, — " to a scoundrel whom I hardly know how to characterize aright — in the presence of a clergyman. Two years ago — doubtless your correspondent has written — my wife and daughter (they were then abroad without me) met him in Paris; and he won the poor child's affection. My wife's judgment was also swayed in his favor, — against her first impulse of distrust; but when I saw him, I could not endure him. Yet I was helpless : my girl's happiness was bound up in him ; all that I could do was to insist upon delay. He was an American, well related, unobjectionable by all the tests which society can apply, and ſ might have had to wait long for the proofs that an accident gave me against him. The man's whole soul was rotten ; at the time he had wound himself into my poor girl's innocent heart, a woman was living who had the just and perhaps the legal claim of a wife upon him ; he was a felon besides, — a felon shielded through pity for his friends by the man whose name he had forged ; he was of course a liar and a coward : I beat him with my stick, sir. Ah ! I made him confess his infamy under his own hand, and then " — the General advances defiantly upon Cummings, who unconsciously retires a pace — " and then I compelled him to break with my daughter. Do you think I did right ? "

Cummings : " I don't exactly understand."

General Wyatt : " Why, sir, it happens often enough in this shabby world that a man gains a poor girl's love, and then jilts her. I chose what I thought the less terrible sorrow for my child. I could not tell her how filthily unworthy he was without bringing to her pure heart a sense of intolerable contamination; I could not endure to speak of it even to my wife. It seemed better that they should both suffer such wrong as a broken engagement might bring them than that they should know what I knew. He was master of the part, and played it well; he showed himself to them simply a heartless scoundrel, and he remains in my power, an outcast now and a convict whenever I will. My story, as it seems to be, is well known in Paris; but the worst is unknown. I choose still that it shall be thought my girl was the victim of a dastardly slight, and I bear with her and her mother the insolent pity with which the world visits such sorrow." He pauses, and then brokenly resumes: "The affair has not turned out as I hoped, in the little I could hope from it. My trust that the blow, which must sink so deeply into her heart, would touch her pride, and that this would help her to react against it, was mistaken. In such things it appears a woman has no pride; I did not know it; we men are different. The blow crushed her; that was all. Sometimes I am afraid that I must yet try the effect of the whole truth upon her; that I must try if the knowledge of all his baseness cannot restore to her the self-respect which the wrong done herself seems to have robbed her of. And yet I tremble lest the sense of his fouler shame — I may be fatally temporizing; but in her present state, I dread any new shock for her; it may be death — I " — He pauses again, and sets his lips firmly; all at once he breaks into a sob. "I — I beg your pardon, sir."

Cummings: "Don't! You wrong yourself and me. I have seen Miss Wyatt; but I hope" —

General Wyatt: "You have seen her ghost. You have not seen the radiant creature that was once alive. Well, sir; enough of this. There is little left to trouble you with. We landed eight days ago, and I have since been looking about for some place in which my daughter could hide herself; I can't otherwise suggest her morbid sensitiveness, her terror of people. This region was highly commended to me for its healthfulness; but

I have come upon this house by chance. I understood that it was empty, and I thought it more than probable that we might pass the autumn months here unmolested by the presence of any one belonging to our world, if not in entire seclusion. At the best, my daughter would hardly have been able to endure another change at once ; so far as anything could give her pleasure, the beauty and the wild quiet of the region had pleased her, but she is now quite prostrated, sir, " —

Cummings, definitively : "My friend will go away at once. There is nothing else for it."

General Wyatt : " That is too much to ask."

Cummings : " I won't conceal my belief that he will think so. But there can be no question with him when " —

General Wyatt : " When you tell him our story ? " After a moment : " Yes, he has a right to know it — as the rest of the world knows it. You must tell him, sir."

Cummings, gently : " No, he need know nothing beyond the fact of this resemblance to some one painfully associated with your past lives. He is a man whose real tenderness of heart would revolt from knowledge that could inflict further sorrow upon you."

General Wyatt: "Sir, will you convey to this friend of yours an old man's very humble apology, and sincere prayer for his forgiveness?"

Cummings: "He will not exact anything of that sort. The evidence of misunderstanding will be clear to him at a word from me."

General Wyatt: "But he has a right to this explanation from my own lips, and — Sir, I am culpably weak. But now that I have missed seeing him here, I confess that I would willingly avoid meeting him. The mere sound of his voice, as I heard it before I saw him, in first coming upon you, was enough to madden me. Can you excuse my senseless dereliction to him?"

Cummings: "I will answer for him."

General Wyatt: "Thanks. It seems monstrous that I should be asking and accepting these great favors. But you are doing a deed of charity to a helpless man utterly beggared in pride." He chokes with emotion, and does not speak for a moment. "Your friend is also — he is not also — a clergyman ?"

Cummings, smiling : "No.   He is a painter."

General Wyatt : "Is he a man of note ?   Succesful in his profession ?"

Cummings : "Not yet.   But that is certain to come."

General Wyatt : "He is poor ?"

Cummings : "He is a young painter."

General Wyatt : "Sir, excuse me.   Had he planned to remain here some time, yet ?"

Cummings, reluctantly : "He has been sketching here.   He had expected to stay through October."

General Wyatt : "You make the sacrifice hard to accept — I beg your pardon !   But I must accept it.   I am bound hand and foot."

Cummings : "I am sorry to have been obliged to tell you this."

General Wyatt : "I obliged you, sir ; I obliged you.   Give me your advice, sir ; you know your friend.   What shall I do ?   I am not rich.   I don't belong to a branch of the government service in which people enrich themselves. But I have my pay; and if your friend could sell me the pictures he 's been painting here " —

Cummings: " That 's quite impossible. There is no form in which I could propose such a thing to a man of his generous pride."

General Wyatt: " Well, then, sir, I must satisfy myself as I can to remain his debtor. Will you kindly undertake to tell him ? "

An Elderly Serving-Woman, who appears timidly and anxiously at the right-hand door: " General Wyatt."

General Wyatt, with a start: "Yes, Mary! Well ?"

Mary, in vanishing: " Mrs. Wyatt wishes to speak with you."

General Wyatt, going up to Cummings: " I must go, sir. I leave unsaid what I cannot even try to say." He offers his hand.

Cummings, grasping the proffered hand: "Everything is understood." But as Mr. Cummings returns from following General Wyatt to the door, his face does not confirm the entire security of his words. He looks anxious and perturbed, and when he has taken up his hat and stick, he stands pondering absent-mindedly. At last he puts on his hat and starts briskly toward the door. Before he reaches it, he encounters Bartlett, who advances abruptly into the room. "Oh! I was going to look for you."

VI

CUMMINGS *and* BARTLETT.

Bartlett, sulkily: "Were you?" He walks, without looking at Cummings, to where his paint- er's paraphernalia are lying, and begins to pick them up.

Cummings: "Yes." In great embarrassment: "Bartlett, General Wyatt has been here."

Bartlett, without looking round: "Who is Gen- eral Wyatt?"

Cummings: "I mean the gentleman who — whom you would n't wait to see."

Bartlett: "Um!" He has gathered the things into his arms, and is about to leave the room.

Cummings, in great distress: "Bartlett, Bart- lett! Don't go! I implore you, if you have any regard for me whatever, to hear what I have to say. It's boyish, it's cruel, it's cowardly to be- have as you 're doing!"

Bartlett: "Anything more, Mr. Cummings? I give you benefit of clergy."

Cummings: "I take it — to denounce your proceeding as something that you 'll always be sorry for and ashamed of."

Bartlett: "Oh! Then, if you have quite freed your mind, I think I may go."

Cummings: "No, no! You must n't go. Don't go, my dear fellow. Forgive me! I know how insulted you feel, but upon my soul it 's all a mistake, — it is, indeed. General Wyatt" — Bartlett falters a moment and stands as if irresolute whether to stay and listen or push on out of the room — "the young lady — I don't know how to begin!"

Bartlett, relenting a little: "Well? I 'm sorry for *you*, Cummings. I left a very awkward business to you, and it was n't yours, either. As for General Wyatt, as he chooses to call himself" —

Cummings, in amaze: " *Call* himself? It 's his name!"

Bartlett: "Oh, very likely! So is King David his name, when he happens to be in a Scriptural craze. What explanation have you been commissioned to make me? What apology?"

Cummings: "The most definite, the most satisfactory. You resemble in a most extraordinary manner a man who has inflicted an abominable wrong upon these people, a treacherous and cowardly villain " —

Bartlett, in a burst of fury: "Stop! Is that your idea of an apology, an explanation? Isn't it enough that I should be threatened, and vilified, and have people fainting at the sight of me, but I must be told by way of reparation that it all happens because I look like a rascal?"

Cummings: "My dear friend! Do listen to me!"

Bartlett: "No, sir, I won't listen to you! I've listened too much! What right, I should like to know, have they to find this resemblance in me? And do they suppose that I'm going to be placated by being told that they treat me like a rogue because I look like one? It's a little too much. A man calls 'Stop Thief' after me and expects me to be delighted when he tells me I look like a thief! The reparation is an additional insult. I don't choose to know that they fancy this infamous resemblance in me. Their pretending it is an outrage; and your reporting it to me is an offense. Will you tell them what I say? Will you tell this General Wyatt and the rest of his Bedlam-broke-loose, that they may all go to the " —

Cummings: " For shame, for shame! You outrage a terrible sorrow! You insult a trouble sore to death! You trample upon an anguish that should be sacred to your tears!"

Bartlett, resting his elbow on the corner of the piano: " What — what do you mean, Cummings?"

Cummings: " What do I mean? What you are not worthy to know! I mean that these people, against whom you vent your stupid rage, are worthy of angelic pity. I mean that by some disastrous mischance you resemble to the life, in tone, manner, and feature, the wretch who won that poor girl's heart, and then crushed it; who — Bartlett, look here! These are the people — this is the young lady — of whom my friend wrote me from Paris; do you understand?"

Bartlett, in a dull bewilderment: "No, I don't understand."

Cummings: "Why, you know what we were talking of just before they came in; you know what I told you of that cruel business."

Bartlett: "Well?"

Cummings: "Well, this is the young lady" —

Bartlett, dauntedly: "Oh, come, now! You don't expect me to believe that! It is n't a stage-play."

Cummings: "Indeed, indeed, I tell you the miserable truth."

Bartlett: "Do you mean to say that *this* is the young girl who was jilted in that way? Who — Do you mean — Do you intend to tell me — Do you suppose — Cummings" —

Cummings: "Yes, yes, yes!"

Bartlett: "Why, man, she 's in Paris, according to your own showing!"

Cummings: "She was in Paris three weeks ago. They have just brought her home, to help her hide her suffering, as if it were her shame, from all who know it. They are in this house by chance, but they are here. I mean what I say. You *must* believe it, shocking and wild as it is."

Bartlett, after a prolonged silence in which he

seems trying to realize the fact: "If you were a man capable of such a ghastly joke — but that's impossible." He is silent again, as before. "And I — What did you say about me? That I look like the man who" — He stops and stares into Cummings's face without speaking, as if he were trying to puzzle the mystery out; then, with fallen head, he muses in a voice of devout and reverent tenderness: "That — that — broken — lily! Oh!" With a sudden start he flings his burden upon the closed piano, whose hidden strings hum with the blow, and advances upon Cummings: "And you can *tell* it? Shame on *you!* It ought to be known to no one upon earth! And you — you show that gentle creature's death-wound to teach something like human reason to a surly dog like me? Oh, it's monstrous! I *was n't* worth it. Better have let me go, where I would, how I would. What did it matter what I thought or said? And I — I look like that devil, do I? I have his voice, his face, his movement? Cummings, you 've over-avenged yourself."

Cummings: "Don't take it that way, Bartlett.

4

It *is* hideous. But I did n't make it so, nor you. It 's a fatality, it 's a hateful chance. But you see now, don't you, Bartlett, how the sight of you must affect them, and how anxious her father must be to avoid you? He most humbly asked your forgiveness, and he hardly knew how to ask that you would not let her see you again. But I told him there could be no question with you; that of course you would prevent it, and at once. I know it 's a great sacrifice to expect you to go " —

Bartlett: " Go? What are you talking about?" He breaks again from the daze into which he had relapsed. "If there 's a hole on the face of the earth where I can hide myself from them, I want to find it. What do you think I 'm made of? Go? I ought to be shot away out of a mortar; I ought to be struck away by lightning! Oh, I can't excuse you, Cummings! The indelicacy, the brutality of telling me that! No, no, — I can't overlook it." He shakes his head and walks away from his friend; then he returns, and bends on him a look of curious inquiry. "Am I really such a ruffian " — he speaks very gently, almost meekly,

now — " that you did n't believe anything short of
that would bring me to my senses? Who told
you this of her? "

Cummings: " Her father."

Bartlett: " Oh, that 's too loathsome! Had the
man no soul, no mercy? Did he think me such a
consummate beast that nothing less would drive me
away? Yes, he did! Yes, I made him think so!
Oh! " He hangs his head and walks away with a
shudder.

Cummings: " I don't know that he did you that
injustice; but I 'm afraid *I* did. I was at my wits'
end."

Bartlett, very humbly: " Oh, I don't know that
you were wrong."

Cummings: " I suppose that his anxiety for her
life made it comparatively easy for him to speak of
the hurt to her pride. She can't be long for this
world."

Bartlett: " No, she had the dying look! " After
a long pause, in which he has continued to wander
aimlessly about the room: " Cummings, is it necessary that you should tell him you told me? "

Cummings: "You know I hate concealments of any kind, Bartlett."

Bartlett: "Oh, well; do it, then!"

Cummings: "But I don't know that we shall see him again; and even if we do, I don't see how I can tell him unless he asks. It's rather painful."

Bartlett: "Well, take that little sin on your conscience, if you can. It seems to me too ghastly that I should know what you've told me; it's indecent. Cummings," — after another pause, — "how does a man go about such a thing? How does he contrive to tell the woman whose heart he has won that he does n't care for her, and break the faith that she would have staked her life on? Oh, I know, — women do such things, too; but it's different, by a whole world's difference. A man comes and a man goes, but a woman *stays.* The world is before him after that happens, and we don't think him much of a man if he can't get over it. But she, she has been sought out; she has been made to believe that her smile and her looks are heaven, poor, foolish, helpless idol! her

fears have been laid, all her pretty maidenly tradi-
tions, her proud reserves overcome; she takes him
into her inmost soul, — to find that his love is a
lie, a lie! Imagine it! She can't do anything.
She can't speak. She can't move as long as she
lives. She must stay where she has been left, and
look and act as if nothing had happened. Oh,
good Heaven! And I, *I* look like a man who
could do that!" After a silence: "I feel as if
there were blood on me!" He goes to the piano,
and gathering up his things turns about towards
Cummings again: " Come, man; I'm going. It's
sacrilege to stay an instant, — to exist."

Cummings: " Don't take it in that way, Bartlett. I blame myself very much for not having
spared you in what I said. I wouldn't have told
you of it, if I could have supposed that an acci-
dental resemblance of the sort would distress you
so."

Bartlett, contritely: "You had to tell me. I
forced you to extreme measures. I'm quite worthy to look like him. Good Lord! I suppose I
should be capable of his work." He moves to-

wards the door with his burden, but before he reaches it General Wyatt, from the corridor, meets him with an air of confused agitation. Bartlett halts awkwardly, and some of the things slip from his hold to the floor.

VII.

General Wyatt, Cummings, *and* Bartlett.

General Wyatt: " Sir, I am glad to see you."
He pronounces the civility with a manner evidently affected by the effort to reconcile Bartlett's
offensive personal appearance with his own sense
of duty. " I — I was sorry to miss you before;
and now I wish — Your friend " — referring with
an inquiring glance to Cummings — " has explained
to you the cause of our very extraordinary behavior, and I hope you " —

Bartlett: " Mr. Cummings has told me that I
have the misfortune to resemble some one with
whom you have painful associations. That is quite
enough and entirely justifies you. I am going at
once, and I trust you will forgive my rudeness
in absenting myself a moment ago. I have a bad
temper; but I never could forgive myself if I had

forced my friend "—he turns and glares warningly at Cummings, who makes a faint pantomime of conscientious protest as Bartlett proceeds — " to hear anything more than the mere fact from you. No, no,"— as General Wyatt seems about to speak, — " it would be atrocious in me to seek to go behind it. I wish to know nothing more." Cummings gives signs of extreme unrest at being made a party to this tacit deception, and General Wyatt, striking his palms hopelessly together, walks to the other end of the room. Bartlett touches the fallen camp-stool with his foot. " Cummings, will you be kind enough to put that on top of this other rubbish ? " He indicates his armful, and as Cummings complies, he says in a swift, fierce whisper: " Her secret is mine. If you dare to hint that you 've told it to me, I 'll — I 'll assault you in your own pulpit." Then to General Wyatt, who is returning toward him : " Good morning, sir."

General Wyatt: "Oh! Ah! Stop! That is, don't go! Really, sir, I don't know what to say. I must have seemed to you like a madman a mo-

ment ago, and now I 've come to play the fool."
Bartlett and Cummings look their surprise and
General Wyatt hurries on: "I asked your friend
to beg you to go away, and now I am here to beg
you to remain. It 's perfectly ridiculous, sir, I
know, and I can say nothing in defense of the
monstrous liberties I have taken. Sir, the matter
is simply this: my daughter's health is so frail that
her life seems to hang by a thread, and I am pow-
erless to do anything against her wish. It may be
a culpable weakness, but I cannot help it. When
I went back to her from seeing your friend, she
immediately divined what my mission had been,
and it had the contrary effect from what I had expected. Well, sir! Nothing would content her
but that I should return and ask you to stay. She
looks upon it as the sole reparation we can make
you."

Bartlett, gently: "I understand that perfectly;
and may I beg you to say that in going away I
thanked her with all my heart, and ventured to
leave her my best wishes?" He bows as if to go.

General Wyatt, detaining him: "Excuse me —

thanks — but — but I am afraid she will not be satisfied with that. She will be satisfied with nothing less than your remaining. It is the whim of a sick child — which I must ask you to indulge. In a few days, sir, I hope we may be able to continue on our way. It would be simply unbearable pain to her to know that we had driven you away, and you must stay to show that you have forgiven the wrong we have done you."

Bartlett: "That's nothing, less than nothing. But I was thinking — I don't care for myself in the matter — that Miss Wyatt is proposing a very unnecessary annoyance for you all. My friend can remain and assure her that I have no feeling whatever about the matter, and in the mean time I can remove — the embarrassment — of my presence."

General Wyatt: "Sir, you are very considerate, very kind. My own judgment is in favor of your course, and yet" —

Cummings: "I think my friend is right, and that when he is gone" —

General Wyatt: "Well, sir! well, sir! It may

be the best way. I think it *is* the best. We will
venture upon it. Sir," — to Bartlett, — "may I
have the honor of taking your hand?" Bartlett
lays down his burden on the piano, and gives his
hand. "Thank you, thank you! You will not regret this goodness. God bless you! May you
always prosper."

Bartlett: "Good-by; and say to Miss Wyatt" —
At these words he pauses, arrested by an incom-
prehensible dismay in General Wyatt's face, and
turning about he sees Cummings transfixed at
the apparition of Miss Wyatt advancing directly
toward himself, while her mother coming behind
her exchanges signals of helplessness and despair
with the General. The young girl's hair, thick and
bronze, has been heaped in hasty but beautiful
masses on her delicate head; as she stands with
fallen eyes before Bartlett, the heavy lashes lie
dark on her pale cheeks, and the blue of her eyes
shows through their transparent lids. She has a
fan with which she makes a weak pretense of play-
ing, and which she puts to her lips as if to hide the
low murmur that escapes from them as she raises
her eyes to Bartlett's face.

VIII.

CONSTANCE, MRS. WYATT, *and the others.*

Constance, with a phantom-like effort at hauteur: "I hope you have been able to forgive the annoyance we caused you, and that you won't let it drive you away." She lifts her eyes with a slow effort, and starts with a little gasp as they fall upon his face, and then remains trembling before him while he speaks.

Bartlett, reverently: "I am to do whatever you wish. I have no annoyance — but the fear that — that" —

Constance, in a husky whisper: "Thanks!" As she turns from him to go back to her mother, she moves so frailly that he involuntarily puts out his hand.

Mrs. Wyatt, starting forward: "No!" But Constance clutches his extended arm with one of her pale hands, and staying herself for a moment lifts her eyes again to his, looks steadily at him with her face half turned upon him, and then, making a slight, sidelong inclination of the head, releases his arm and goes to her mother, who supports her to one of the easy-chairs and kneels beside her when she sinks into it. Bartlett, after an instant of hesitation, bows silently and withdraws, Cummings having already vanished. Constance watches him going, and then hides her face on her mother's neck.

II.

DISTINCTIONS AND DIFFERENCES.

I.

CONSTANCE *and* MRS. WYATT.

Constance: " And he is still here? He is going to stay on, mother?" She reclines in a low folding chair, and languidly rests her head against one of the pillows with which her mother has propped her; on the bright-colored shawl which has been thrown over her lie her pale hands loosely holding her shut fan. Her mother stands half across the parlor from her, and wistfully surveys her work, to see if some touch may not yet be added for the girl's comfort.

Mrs. Wyatt: " Yes, my child. He will stay. He told your father he would stay."

Constance: " That 's very kind of him. He 's very good."

Mrs. Wyatt, seating herself before her daughter: " Do you really wish him to stay? Remember

5

how weak you are, Constance. If you are taking anything upon yourself out of a mistaken sense of duty, of compunction, you are not kind to your poor father or to me. Not that I mean to reproach you."

Constance : " Oh, no. And I am not unkind to you in the way you think. I 'm selfish enough in wishing him to stay. I can't help wanting to see him again and again, — it 's so strange, so strange. All this past week, whenever I 've caught a glimpse of him, it 's been like an apparition ; and whenever he has spoken, it has been like a ghost speaking. But I have n't been afraid since the first time. No, there 's been a dreary comfort in it; you won't understand it; I can't understand it myself; but I know now why people are glad to see their dead in dreams. If the ghost went, there would be nothing."

Mrs. Wyatt : " Constance, you break my heart ! "

Constance : " Yes, I know it; it 's because I 've none." She remains a little space without speaking, while she softly fingers the edges of the fan lying in her lap. " I suppose we shall become more acquainted, if he stays ? "

Mrs. Wyatt: " Why, not necessarily, dear. You need know nothing more of him than you do now. He seems very busy, and not in the least inclined to intrude upon us. Your father thinks him a little odd, but very gentlemanly."

Constance, dreamily: " I wonder what he would think if he knew that the man whom I would have given my life did not find my love worth having? I suppose it *was* worthless; but it seemed so much in the giving; it was that deceived me. He was wiser. Oh, me!" After a silence: " Mother, why was I so different from other girls?"

Mrs. Wyatt: " So different, Constance? You were only different in being lovelier and better than others."

Constance: " Ah, that's the mistake! If that were true, it could never have happened. Other girls, the poorest and plainest, are kept faith with; but I was left. There must have been something about me that made him despise me. Was I silly, mother? Was I too bold, too glad to have him care for me? I was so happy that I couldn't help showing it. May be that displeased him. I must

have been dull and tiresome. And I suppose I
was somehow repulsive, and at last he could n't
bear it any longer and had to break with me. Did
I dress queerly? I know I looked ridiculous at
times; and people laughed at me before him."

Mrs. Wyatt: "Oh, Constance, Constance! Can't
you understand that it was his unworthiness alone,
his wicked heartlessness?"

Constance, with gentle slowness: "No, I can't
understand that. It happened after we had learned
to know each other so well. If he had been fickle,
it would have happened long before that. It was
something odious in me that he did n't see at first.
I have thought it out. It seems strange now that
people could ever have tolerated me." Desolately:
" Well, they have their revenge."

Mrs. Wyatt: "Their revenge on *you,* Constance?
What harm did you ever do them, my poor child?
Oh, you must n't let these morbid fancies overcome you. Where is our Constance that used to
be, — our brave, bright girl, that nothing could
daunt, and nothing could sadden?"

Constance, sobbing: "Dead, dead!"

Mrs. Wyatt: "I can't understand! You are so young still, and with the world all before you. Why will you let one man's baseness blacken it all and blight your young life so?" Where is your pride, Constance?"

Constance: "Pride? What have I to do with pride? A thing like me!"

Mrs. Wyatt: "Oh, child, you're pitiless! It seems as if you took a dreadful pleasure in torturing those who love you."

Constance: "You've said it, mother. I do. I know now that I am a vampire, and that it's my hideous fate to prey upon those who are dearest to me. He must have known, he must have felt the vampire in me."

Mrs. Wyatt: "Constance!"

Constance: "But at least I can be kind to those who care nothing for me. Who is this stranger? He must be an odd kind of man to forgive us. What is he, mother?—if he is anything in himself; he seems to me only a likeness, not a reality."

Mrs. Wyatt: "He is a painter, your father says."

Mrs. Wyatt gives a quick sigh of relief, and makes haste to confirm the direction of the talk away from Constance: "He is painting some landscapes, here. That friend of his who went to-day is a cousin of your father's old friend, Major Cummings. He's a minister."

Constance: "What is the painter's name? Not that it matters. But I must call him something if I meet him again."

Mrs. Wyatt: "Mr. Bartlett."

Constance: "Oh, yes, I forgot." She falls into a brooding silence. "I wonder if *he* will despise me — if he will be like in that, too?" Mrs. Wyatt sighs patiently. "Why do you mind what I say, mother? I'm not worth it. I must talk on, or else go mad with the mystery of what has been. We were so happy; he was so good to me, so kind; there was nothing but papa's not seeming to like him; and then suddenly, in an instant, he turns and strikes me down! Yes, it was like a deadly blow. If you don't let me believe that it was because he saw all at once that I was utterly unworthy, I can't believe in anything."

Mrs. Wyatt : " Hush, Constance ; you don't know what you 're saying."

Constance : " Oh, I know too well ! And now this stranger, who is so like him — who has all his looks, who has his walk, who has his voice, — won't he have his insight, too ? I had better show myself for what I am, at once — weak, stupid, selfish, false ; it 'll save me the pain of being found out. Pain ? Oh, I 'm past hurting ! Why do you cry, mother ? I 'm not worth your tears."

Mrs. Wyatt : " You 're all the world to us, Constance ; you know it, child. Your poor father "—

Constance : " Does papa really like me ? "

Mrs. Wyatt : " Constance ! "

Constance : " No; but why should he ? He never liked *him ;* and sometimes I 've wondered, if it was n't papa's not liking him that first set him against me. Of course, it was best he should find me out, but still I can't keep from thinking that if he had never *begun* to dislike me ! I noticed from the first that after papa had been with us he was cold and constrained. Mother, I had better say it: I don't believe I love papa as I

ought. There's something in my heart — some
hardness — against him when he's kindest to me.
If he had only been kinder to *him*" —

Mrs. Wyatt : "Kinder to *him ?* Constance, you
drive me wild ! Kind to a wolf, kind to a snake !
Kind to the thief who has robbed us of all that
made our lives dear; who stole your love, and
then your hope, your health, your joy, your pride,
your peace ! And you think your father might
have been kinder. to *him !* Constance, you were
our little girl when the war began, — the last of
brothers and sisters that had died. You seemed
given to our later years to console and comfort us
for those that had been taken ; and you were *so*
bright and gay ! All through those dreadful days
and months and years you were our stay and hope,
— mine at home, his in the field. Our letters
were full of you, — like young people's with their
first child ; all that you did and said I had to tell
him, and then he had to talk it over in his answers
back. When he came home at last after the peace
— can you remember it, Constance ? "

Constance : "I can remember a little girl that

ran down the street, and met an officer on horse-back. He was all tanned and weather-beaten; he sat his horse at the head of his troop like a statue of bronze. When he saw her come running, dan-cing down the street, he leaped from his horse and caught her in his arms, and hugged her close and kissed her, and set her all crying and laughing in his saddle, and walked on beside her; and the men burst out with a wild yell, and the ragged flags flapped, over her, and the music flashed out"— She rises in her chair with the thrill of her recol-lection; her voice comes free and full, and her pale cheeks flush; suddenly she sinks back upon the pil-lows: "Was it really I, mother?"

Mrs. Wyatt: "Yes, it was you, Constance. And do you remember all through your school-days, how proud and fond he was of you? what presents and feasts and pleasures he was always making you? I thought he would spoil you; he took you everywhere with him, and wanted to give you everything. When I saw you growing up with his pride and quick temper, I trembled, but I felt safe when I saw that you had his true and tender heart, too. You can never know what a pang it cost him to part with you when we went abroad, but you can't forget how he met you in Paris?"

Constance: "Oh, no, no! Poor papa!"

Mrs. Wyatt: "Oh, child! And I could tell you something of his bitter despair when he saw the man"—

Constance, wearily: "You need n't tell me. I knew it as soon as they met, without looking at either of them."

Mrs. Wyatt: "And when the worst that he feared came true, he was almost glad, I believe. He thought, and I thought, that your self-respect would come to your aid against such treachery."

Constance: "My self-respect? Now I know you 've not been talking of me."

Mrs. Wyatt, desperately: "Oh, what shall I do?"

Mary, the serving-woman, at the door: "If you please, Mrs. Wyatt, I can't open Miss Constance's hat-box."

Mrs. Wyatt, rising: "Oh, yes. There 's something the matter with the lock. I 'll come, Mary." She looks at Constance.

Constance: "Yes, go, mother. I 'm perfectly well here. I like being alone well enough." As Mrs. Wyatt, after a moment's reluctance, goes out, the girl's heavy eyelids fall, and she lies motionless against her pillows, while the fan, released from her careless hold, slides slowly over the shawl, and drops with a light clash upon the floor. She starts at the sound, and utters a little involuntary cry at sight of Bartlett, who stands irresolute in the doorway on her right. He makes as if to retreat, but at a glance from her he remains.

II.

Bartlett and Constance.

Bartlett, with a sort of subdued gruffness:
"I 'm afraid I disturbed you."

Constance, passively: "No, I think it was my
fan. It fell."

Bartlett: "I 'm glad I can lay the blame on the
fan." He comes abruptly forward and picks it up
for her. She makes no motion to receive it, and
he lays it on her lap.

Constance, starting from the abstraction in which
she has been gazing at him: "Oh! Thanks."

Bartlett, with constraint: "I hope you 're better
this morning?"

Constance: "Yes." She has again fallen into
a dreamy study of him, as unconscious, apparently,
as if he were a picture before her, the effect of
which is to reduce him to a state of immovable

awkwardness. At last he tears himself loose from the spot on which he has been petrifying, and takes refuge in the business which has brought him into the room.

Bartlett : " I came to look for one of my brushes. It must have dropped out of my traps here, the other day." He goes up to the piano and looks about the floor, while Constance's gaze follows him in every attitude and movement. "Ah, here it is! I knew it would escape the broom under the landlady's relaxed régime. If you happen to drop anything in this room, Miss Wyatt, you need n't be troubled; you can always find it just where it fell." Miss Wyatt's fan again slips to the floor, and Bartlett again picks it up and restores it to her: "A case in point."

Constance, blushing faintly: "Don't do it for me. It is n't worth while."

Bartlett, gravely: "It does n't take a great deal of time, and the exercise does me good." Constance faintly smiles, but does not relax her vigilance. "Is n't that light rather strong for you?" He goes to the glass doors opening on the balcony, and offers to draw down one of their shades.

Constance : "It does n't make any difference."

Bartlett, bluffly : "If it 's disagreeable it makes some difference.   Is it disagreeable ? "

Constance : "The light 's strong " — Bartlett dashes the curtain down — "but I could see the mountain."   He pulls the curtain up.

Bartlett : "I beg your pardon."   He again falls into statue-like discomposure under Miss Wyatt's gaze, which does not seek the distant slopes of Ponkwasset, in spite of the lifted curtain.

Constance : "What is the name?   Do you know ? "

Bartlett : "Whose?   Oh ! Ponkwasset.   It 's not a pretty name, but it 's aboriginal.   And it does n't hurt the mountain."   Recovering a partial volition, he shows signs of a purpose to escape, when Miss Wyatt's next question arrests him.

Constance : " Are you painting it, Mr. — Bartlett ? "

Bartlett, with a laugh: "Oh, no, I don't soar so high as mountains; I only lift my eyes to a tree here and there, and a bit of pasture and a few of the lowlier and friendlier sort of rocks."   He now so far effects his purpose as to transfer his unwieldly presence to a lateral position as regards Miss Wyatt. The girl mechanically turns her head upon the pillow and again fixes her sad eyes upon him.

Constance: " Have you ever been up it?"

Bartlett: " Yes, half a dozen times."

Constance: "Is it hard to climb — like the Swiss mountains?"

Bartlett: " *You* must speak for the Swiss mountains after you've tried Ponkwasset, Miss Wyatt. I've never been abroad."

Constance, her large eyes dilating with surprise: "Never been abroad?"

Bartlett: " I enjoy that distinction."

Constance: "Oh! I thought you had been abroad." She speaks with a slow, absent, earnest, accent, regarding him, as always, with a look of wistful bewilderment.

Bartlett, struggling uneasily for his habitual lightness: "I'm sorry to disappoint you, Miss Wyatt. I will go abroad as soon as possible. I'm going out in a boat this morning to work at a bit on the point of the island yonder, and I'll take lessons in sea-faring." Bartlett, managing at last to get fairly behind Miss Wyatt's chair, indulges himself in a long, low sigh of relief, and taking out his handkerchief rubs his face with it.

Constance, with sudden, meek compunction: " I 've been detaining you."

Bartlett, politely coming forward again: "Oh, no, not at all! I'm afraid I've tired *you.*"

Constance: "No, I 'm glad to have you stay." In the unconscious movement necessary to follow Bartlett in his changes of position, the young girl has loosened one of the pillows that prop her head. It slowly disengages itself and drops to the floor. Bartlett, who has been crushing his brush against the ball of his thumb, gives a start of terror, and looks from Constance to the pillow, and back again to Constance in despair.

Constance: "Never mind." She tries to adjust her head to the remaining pillows, and then desists in evident discomfort.

Bartlett, in great agony of spirit: "I—I 'm afraid you miss it."

Constance: " Oh, no."

Bartlett: " Shall I call your mother, Miss Wyatt ? "

Constance: " No. Oh, no. She will be here
presently. Thank you so much." Bartlett eyes
the pillow in renewed desperation.

Bartlett: " Do you think — do you suppose I
could " — Recklessly : " Miss Wyatt, let *me* put
back that pillow for you ! "

Constance, promptly, with a little flush : " Why,
you 're very good ! I 'm ashamed to trouble you."
As she speaks, she raises her head, and lifts herself forward slightly by help of the chair-arms ; two
more pillows topple out, one on either side, unknown to her.

Bartlett, maddened by the fresh disaster : " Good
Lord ! " He flings himself wildly upon the first
pillow, and crams it into the chair behind Miss
Wyatt ; then without giving his courage time to
flag, he seizes the others, and packs them in on top
of it : " Will that do ? " He stands hot and flushed,
looking down upon her, as she makes a gentle attempt to adjust herself to the mass.

Constance: "Oh, perfectly." She puts her hand behind her and feebly endeavors to modify Bartlett's arrangement.

Bartlett: "What is it?"

Constance: "Oh — nothing. Ah — would — would you draw this one a little — toward you? So! Thanks. And that one — out a little on the —other side? You 're very kind; that 's right. And this one under my neck — lift it up a little? Ah, thank you ever so much." Bartlett, in a fine frenzy, obeying these instructions, Miss Wyatt at last reposes herself against the pillows, looks up into his embarrassed face, and deeply blushes; then she turns suddenly white, and weakly catching up her fan she passes it once or twice before her face, and lets it fall: "I 'm a little — faint." Bartlett seizes the fan, and after a moment of silent self-dedication kneels down beside her chair, and fans her.

Constance, after a moment; "Thanks, thanks. You are very good. I 'm better now. I 'm ashamed to have troubled you. But I seem to live only to give trouble."

Bartlett, with sudden deep tenderness; "Oh, Miss Wyatt, you must n't say that. I 'm sure I — we all — that is — shall I call your mother *now*, Miss Wyatt?"

Constance, after a deep breath, firmly: "No. I 'm quite well, now. She is busy. But I know I 'm keeping *you* from your work," — with ever so slight a wan little smile. "I must n't do that."

Bartlett: "Oh, you 're not *keeping* me! There 's no hurry. I can work later just as well."

Constance: "Then," — with a glance at his devout posture, of which Bartlett has himself become quite unconscious, — "won't you sit down, Mr. Bartlett?"

Bartlett, restored to consciousness and confusion: "Thanks; I think it will be better." He rises, and in his embarrassment draws a chair to the spot on which he has been kneeling and sits down very close to her. He keeps the fan in his hand, as he talks: "It 's rather nice out there, Miss Wyatt, — there on the island. You must be rowed out as soon as you can stand it. The General would like it."

Constance: "Is it a large place, the island?"

Bartlett: "About two acres, devoted exclusively to golden-rod and granite. The fact is, I was going to make a little study of golden-rod and granite, there. You shall visit the Fortunate Isle in my sketch, this afternoon, and see whether you'd like to go, really. People camp out there in the summer. Who knows, but if you keep on — gaining — this way, you may yet feel like camping out there yourself before you go away? You do begin to feel better, don't you? Everybody cries up this air."

Constance: "It's very pleasant; it seems fine and pure. Is the island a pretty place?"

Bartlett, glancing out at it over his shoulder: "Well, you get the best of it from the parlor window, here. Not that it's so bad when you're on it; there's a surly, frugal, hard-headed kind of beauty about it, — like the local human nature, — and it has its advantages. If you were camping out there, you could almost provision yourself from the fish and wild fowl of the surrounding waters, —supposing any of your party liked to fish or shoot. Does your father like shooting?"

Constance: "No, I don't believe he cares for it."

Bartlett: "I'm glad of that. I shall be spared the painful hospitality of pointing out the best places for ducks." At an inquiring look from Constance: "I'm glad for their sakes, not mine: *I* don't want to kill them."

Constance, with grave mistrust: "Not like shooting?"

Bartlett: "No, I think it's the sneakingest sort of assassination; it's the pleasure of murder without the guilt. If you must kill, you ought to be man enough to kill something that you'll suffer remorse for. Do you consider those atrocious sentiments, Miss Wyatt? I assure you that they're entirely my own."

Constance, blankly: "I was n't thinking — I was thinking — I supposed you liked shooting."

Bartlett, laughing uneasily: "How did you get that impression?"

Constance, evasively: "I thought all gentlemen did."

Bartlett: "They do, in this region. It's the only thing that can comfort them in affliction. The other day our ostler's brother lost his sweetheart, —she died, poor girl,—and the ostler and another friend had him over here to cheer him up. They took him to the stable, and whittled round among the stalls with him half the forenoon, and let him rub down some of the horses; they stood him out among the vegetables and let him gather some of the new kind of potato-bugs; they made him sit in the office with his feet on top of the stove; they played billiards with him; but he showed no signs of res- ignation till they borrowed three squirrel-guns and started with him to the oak woods yonder. That seemed to 'fetch' him. You should have seen them trudging off together with their guns all aslant,— this way,—the stricken lover in the middle!" Bart- lett rises to illustrate, and then at the deepening solemnity of Constance's face he desists in sudden dismay: "Miss Wyatt, I've shocked you!"

Constance: "Oh, no—no!"

Bartlett: "It *was* shocking. I wonder how I could do it! I—I thought it would amuse you."

Constance, mournfully: "It did, thank you, very much." After a pause: "I did n't know you liked —joking."

Bartlett: " Ah! I don't believe I do — all kinds. Good Lord — I beg your pardon." Bartlett turns away, with an air of guilty consciousness, and goes to the window and looks out; Constance's gaze following him: "It 's a wonderful day!" He comes back toward her: " What a pity you could n't be carried there in your chair!"

Constance: " I 'm not equal to that, yet." Presently: " Then you — like — nature?"

Bartlett: " Why, that 's mere shop in a landscape painter. I get my bread and butter by her. At least I ought to have some feeling of gratitude."

Constance, hastily: " Of course, of course. It 's very stupid of me, asking."

Bartlett, with the desperate intention of grappling with the situation: " I see you have a passion for formulating, classifying people, Miss Wyatt. That 's all very well, if one's characteristics were not so very characteristic of everybody else. But I generally find in my moments of self-consciousness, when I 've gone round priding myself that such and such traits are my peculiar property, that the first man I meet has them all and as many more, and is n't the least proud of them. I dare say you don't see anything very strange in them, so far."

Constance, musingly: "Oh, yes; very strange indeed. They 're all — wrong!"

Bartlett: "Well! I don't know — I 'm very sorry — Then you consider it wrong not to like shooting and to be fond of joking and nature, and " — .

Constance, bewilderedly: "Wrong? Oh, no!"

Bartlett: "Oh, I 'm glad to hear it. But you just said it was."

Constance, slowly recalling herself, with a painful blush, at last: "I meant — I meant I did n't expect any of those things of you."

Bartlett, with a smile: "Well, on reflection, I don't know that I did, either. I think they must have come without being expected. Upon my word, I 'm tempted to propose something very ridiculous."

Constance, uneasily: "Yes? What is that?"

Bartlett: "That you 'll let me try to guess *you* out. I 've failed so miserably in my own case, that I feel quite encouraged."

Constance, morbidly : " I 'm not worth the trouble of guessing out."

Bartlett : " That means no. You always mean no by yes, because you can't bear to say no. That is the mark of a very deep and darkling nature. I feel that I *could* go on and read your mind perfectly, but I 'm afraid to do it. Let 's get back to myself. I can't allow that you 've failed to read my mind aright ; I think you were careless about it. Will you give your intuitions one more chance ? "

Constance, with an anxious smile : " Oh, yes."

Bartlett : " All those traits and tastes which we both find so unexpected in me are minor matters at the most. The great test question remains. If you answer it rightly, you prove yourself a mind-reader of wonderful power ; if you miss it — The question is simply this : Do I like smoking ? "

Constance, instantly, with a quick, involuntary pressure of her handkerchief to her delicate nostrils : " Oh, yes, indeed ! "

Bartlett, daunted and reddening : " Miss Wyatt, you have been deluding me. You are really a mind-reader of great subtlety."

Constance: " I don't know — I can't say that it was *mind*-reading exactly." She lifts her eyes to his, and in his embarrassment he passes his hand over his forehead and then feels first in one pocket and then in the other for his handkerchief; suddenly he twitches it forth, and with it a pipe, half a dozen cigars, and a pouch of smoking tobacco, which fly in different directions over the floor. As he stoops in dismay and sweeps together these treasures, she cries: " Oh, it did n't need all *that* to prove it!" and breaks into a wild, helpless laugh, and striving to recover herself with many little moans and sighs behind her handkerchief, laughs on and on: " Oh, don't! I ought n't! Oh dear, oh dear!" When at last she lies spent with her reluctant mirth, and uncovers her face, Bartlett is gone, and it is her mother who stands over her, looking down at her with affectionate misgiving.

III.

Mrs. Wyatt *and* Constance.

Mrs. Wyatt: " Laughing, Constance ? "

Constance, with a burst of indignant tears : " Yes, yes! Is n't it shocking? It 's horrible! He made me."

Mrs. Wyatt: " He? "

Constance, beginning to laugh again: " Mr. Bartlett; he 's been here. Oh, I *wish* I *would n't* be so silly ! "

Mrs. Wyatt: " Made you? How could he make *you* laugh, poor child ? "

Constance: " Oh, it 's a long story. It was all through my bewilderment at his resemblance. It confused me. I kept thinking it was *he,* — as if it were some dream, — and whenever this one mentioned some trait of his that totally differed from *his,* don't you know, I got more and more confused, and — mamma!"—with sudden desolation—"I know he knows all about it!"

Mrs. Wyatt: "I am sure he does n't. Mr. Cummings only told him that his resemblance was a painful association. He assured your father of this, and would n't hear a word more. I'm certain you're wrong. But what made you think he knows?"

Constance, solemnly: "He behaved just as if he did n't."

Mrs. Wyatt: "Ah, you can't judge from that, my dear." Impressively: "Men are very different."

Constance, doubtfully: "Do you think so, mamma?"

Mrs. Wyatt: "I'm certain of it."

Constance, after a pause: "Mamma, will you help take this shawl off my feet? I am so warm. I think I should like to walk about a little. Can you see the island from the gallery?"

Mrs. Wyatt: "Do you think you'd better try to leave your chair, Constance?"

Constance: "Yes, I'm stronger this morning. And I shall never gain, lounging about this way."

She begins to loose the wraps from her feet, and Mrs. Wyatt coming doubtfully to her aid she is presently freed. She walks briskly toward the sofa, and sits down quite erectly in the corner of it. "There! that's pleasanter. I get so tired of being a burden." She is silent, and then she begins softly and wearily to laugh again.

Mrs. Wyatt, smiling curiously: "What is it, Constance? I don't at all understand what made you laugh."

Constance: "Why, don't you know? Several times after I had been surprised that he did n't like this thing, and had n't that habit and the other, he noticed it, and pretended that it was an attempt at mind-reading, and then all at once he turned and said I must try once more, and he asked, 'Do I like smoking?' and I said instantly, 'Oh, yes!' Why, it was like having a whole tobacconist's shop in the same room with you from the moment he came in; and of course he understood what I meant, and blushed, and then felt for his handkerchief, and pulled it out, and discharged a perfect volley of pipes and tobacco, that seemed to be tangled up in it, all over the floor, and then I began to laugh — so silly, so disgusting, so perfectly flat! and I thought I should *die*, it was so ridiculous!. and — Oh, dear, I'm beginning again!" She hides her face in her handkerchief and leans her head on the back of the sofa: "Say something, *do* something to stop me, mother!" She stretches an imploring left hand toward the elder lady, who still remains apparently but half convinced of any reason for mirth, when General Wyatt, hastily entering, pauses in abrupt irresolution at the spectacle of Constance's passion.

IV.

GENERAL WYATT, CONSTANCE, *and* MRS. WYATT.

Constance: "*Oh*, ha, ha, ha! Oh, *ha*, ha, ha, ha!"

General Wyatt: "Margaret! Constance!" At the sound of his voice, Constance starts up with a little cry, and stiffens into an attitude of ungracious silence, without looking at her father, who turns with an expression of pain toward her mother.

Mrs. Wyatt: "Yes, James. We were laughing at something Constance had been telling me about Mr. Bartlett. Tell your father, Constance."

Constance, coldly, while she draws through her hand the handkerchief which she has been pressing to her eyes: "I don't think it would amuse papa." She passes her hand across her lap, and does not lift her heavy eyelashes.

Mrs. Wyatt, caressingly: "Oh, yes, it would; I'm sure it would."

Constance: "You can tell it then, mamma."

Mrs. Wyatt: "No; you, my dear. You tell it so funnily; and" — in a lower tone — "it's so long since your father heard you laugh."

Constance: "There was nothing funny in it. It was disgusting. I was laughing from nervousness."

Mrs. Wyatt: "Why, Constance" —

General Wyatt: Never mind, Margaret. Another time will do." He chooses to ignore the coldness of his daughter's bearing toward himself. "I came to see if Constance were not strong enough to go out on the lake this morning. The boats are very good, and the air is so fine that I think she'll be the better for it. Mr. Bartlett is going out to the island to sketch, and" —

Constance: "I don't care to go."

Mrs. Wyatt: "Do go, my daughter! I know it will do you good."

Constance: "I am not strong enough."

Mrs. Wyatt: "But you said you were better, just now; and you should yield to your father's judgment."

Constance: "I will do whatever papa bids me."

General Wyatt: " I don't bid you. Margaret, I think I will go out with Mr. Bartlett. We will be back at dinner." He turns and leaves the room without looking again at Constance.

7

V.

CONSTANCE *and* MRS. WYATT; *then* BARTLETT.

Mrs. Wyatt: "Oh, Constance! How can you treat your father so coldly? You will suffer some day for the pain you give him!"

Constance: "Suffer? No, I'm past that. I've exhausted my power of suffering."

Mrs. Wyatt: "You have n't exhausted your power of making others suffer."

Constance, crouching listlessly down upon the sofa: "I told you that I lived only to give pain. But it's my fate, not my will. Nothing but that can excuse me."

Mrs. Wyatt, wringing her hands: "Oh, oh! Well, then, give *me* pain if you must torment somebody. But spare your father, — spare the heart that loves you so tenderly, you unhappy girl."

Constance, with hardness: "Whenever I see

papa, my first thought is, If he had not been so harsh and severe, it might never have happened! What can I care for his loving me when he hated *him?* Oh, *I* will do my duty, mother; *I* will obey; I *have* obeyed, and I know how. Papa can't demand anything of me *now* that is n't easy. I have forgiven everything, and if you give me time I can forget. I *have* forgotten. I have been laughing at something so foolish, it ought to make me cry for shame."

Mrs. Wyatt: " Constance, you try me beyond all endurance! You talk of forgiving, you talk of forgetting, you talk of that wretch! Forgive *him*, forget *him*, if you can. If he had been half a man, if he had ever cared a tithe as much for you as for himself, all the hate of all the fathers in the world could not have driven him from you. You talk of obeying " —

Mary, the serving woman, flying into the room: " Oh, please, Mrs. Wyatt! There are four men carrying somebody up the hill. And General Wyatt just went down, and I can't see him anywhere, and " —

Mrs. Wyatt : "You 're crazy, Mary! He has n't been gone a moment; there is n't time; it can't be he!" Mrs. Wyatt rushes to the gallery that over-looks the road to verify her hope or fear, and then out of one of the doors into the corridor, while Constance springs frantically to her feet and runs toward the other door.

Constance : "Oh, yes, yes! It's papa! It's my dear, good, kind papa! He's dead; he's drowned; I drove him away; I murdered him! Ah-h-h-h!" She shrinks back with a shriek at sight of Bartlett, whose excited face appears at the door: "Go! It was you, *you* who made me hate my father! You made me kill him and now I abhor you! I"—

Bartlett : "Wait! Hold on! What is it all?"

Constance : "Oh, forgive me! I did n't mean— I did n't know it was you, sir! But where *is* he? Oh, take me to him! Is he dead?" She seizes his arm, and clings to it trembling.

Bartlett : "Dead? No, he is n't dead. He was knocked over by a team coming behind him down the hill, and was slightly bruised. There's no cause for alarm. He sent me to tell you; they 've carried him to your rooms."

Constance: "Oh, thank Heaven!" She bows her head with a sob, upon his shoulder, and then lifts her tearful eyes to his : "Help me to get to him! I am weak." She totters and Bartlett mechanically passes a supporting arm about her. "Help me, and don't—don't leave me!" She moves with him a few paces toward the door, her head drooping; but all at once she raises her face again, stares at him, stiffly releases herself, and with a long look of reproach walks proudly away to the other door, by which she vanishes without a word.

Bartlett, remaining planted, with a bewildered glance at his empty arm : "Well, I wonder who and what and where I am !"

III.

NOT AT ALL LIKE.

BARTLETT *and* CUMMINGS.

Bartlett: "Six weeks since you were here? I should n't have thought that." Bartlett's easel stands before the window, in the hotel parlor; he has laid a tint upon the canvas, and has retired a few paces for the effect, his palette and mahl-stick in hand, and his head carried at a critical angle. Cummings, who has been doing the duty of art-culture by the picture, regards it with renewed interest. Bartlett resumes his work: "Pretty good, Cummings?"

Cummings: "Capital! The blue of that distance"—

Bartlett, with a burlesque sigh: "Ah, I looked into my heart and painted for *that!* Well, you find me still here, Cummings, and apparently more at home than ever. The landlord has devoted this parlor to the cause of art, — makes the transients use the lower parlor, now, — and we have this all to ourselves: Miss Wyatt sketches, you know. Her mother brings her sewing, and the General his bruises; he has n't quite scrambled up, yet, from that little knock-down of his; a man does n't, at his time of life, I believe; and we make this our family-room; and a very queer family we are! Fine old fellow, the General; he 's behaved himself since his accident like a disabled angel, and has n't sworn, — well, anything worth speaking of. Yes, here I am. I suppose it 's all right, but for all I know it may be all wrong." Bartlett sighs in unguarded sincerity. "*I* don't know what I 'm here for. Nature began shutting up shop a fortnight ago at a pretty lively rate, and edging loafers to the door, with every sign of impatience; and yet, here I am, hanging round still. I suppose this glimpse of Indian Summer is some excuse just now; it 's a perfect blessing to the landlord, and he 's making hay — rowen crop — while the sun shines; I 've been with him so long now, I take quite an interest in his prosperity, if eight dollars a week of it *do* come out of me! What is talked of in 'art-circles' down in Boston, brother Cummings?"

Cummings : "Your picture."

Bartlett, inattentively, while he comes up to his canvas, and bestows an infinitesimal portion of paint upon a destitute spot in the canvas: "Don't be sarcastic, Cummings."

Cummings : "I'm not, I assure you."

Bartlett, turning toward him incredulously: "Do you mean to say that The First Gray Hair is liked?"

Cummings: "I do. There hasn't been any picture so much talked of this season."

Bartlett: "Then it's the shameless slop of the name. I should think you'd blush for your part in that swindle. But clergymen have *no* conscience, where they've a chance to do a fellow a kindness, I've observed." He goes up to Cummings with his brush in his mouth, his palette on one hand, and his mahl-stick in the other, and contrives to lay hold of his shoulders with a few disengaged fingers. As Cummings shrinks a little from his embrace: "Oh, don't be afraid; I shan't get any paint on you. You need a whole coat of whitewash, though, you unscrupulous saint!" He returns to his easel. "So The Old Girl — that's what I shall call the picture — is a success, is she? The admiring public ought to see the original elm-tree now; she has n't got a hair, gray or green, on her head; she's perfectly bald. I say, Cummings, how would it do for me to paint a pendant, *The Last Gray Hair?* I might look up a leaf or two on the elm, somewhere: stick it on to the point of twig; they would n't know any better."

Cummings: "The leafless elm would make a good picture, whatever you called it." Bartlett throws back his shaggy head and laughs up at the ceiling. "The fact is, Bartlett, I 've got a little surprise for you."

Bartlett, looking at him askance: "Somebody wanting to chromo The Old Girl? No, no; it is n't quite so bad as that!"

Cummings, in a burst: "They *did* want to chromo it. But it 's sold. They 've got you two hundred dollars for it." Bartlett lays down his brush, palette, and mahl-stick, dusts his fingers, puts them in his pockets, and comes and stands before Cummings, on whom, seated, he bends a curious look.

Bartlett: "And do you mean to tell me, you hardened atheist, that you don't believe in the doctrine of future punishments? What are they going to do with *you* in the next world? And that picture dealer? And *me?* Two hund— It's an outrage! It's— The picture was n't worth fifty, by a stretch of the most charitable imagination! Two hundred d— Why, Cummings, I'll paint no end of Old Girls, First and Last Gray Hairs— I'll flood the market! Two— Good Lord!" Bartlett goes back to his easel, and silently resumes his work. After a while: "Who's been offered up?"

Cummings: "What?"

Bartlett: "Who's the victim? My patron? The noble and discriminating and munificent purchaser of The Old Girl?"

Cummings: "Oh! Mrs. Bellingham. She's going to send it out to her daughter in Omaha."

Bartlett: " Ah ! Mrs. Blake wishes to found an art-museum with that curiosity out there ? Sorry for the Omaha-has." Cummings makes a gesture of impatience. " Well, well ; I won't then, old fellow ! I 'm truly obliged to you. I accept my good fortune with compunction, but with all the gratitude imaginable. I say, Cummings ! "

Cummings: " Well ? "

Bartlett: " What do you think of my taking to high art, — mountains twelve hundred feet above the sea, like this portrait of Ponkwasset?"

Cummings: " I 've always told you that you had only to give yourself scope, — attempt something worthy of your powers" —

Bartlett: " Ah, I thought so. Then you believe that a good big canvas and a good big subject would be the making of me? Well, I 've come round to that idea myself. I used to think that if there was any greatness in me, I could get it into a small picture, like Meissonier or Corot. But I can't. I must have room, like the Yellowstone and Yo-Semite fellows. Don't you think Miss Wyatt is looking wonderfully improved?"

Cummings: "Wonderfully! And how beautiful she is! She looked lovely that first day, in spite of her ghostliness; but now"—

Bartlett: "Yes; a *phantom* of delight is good enough in its way, but a *well woman* is the prettiest, after all. Miss Wyatt sketches, I think I told you."

Cummings: "Yes, you mentioned it."

Bartlett: "Of course. Otherwise, I couldn't possibly have thought of her while I was at work on a great picture like this. She sketches"— Bartlett puts his nose almost on the canvas in the process of bestowing a delicate touch — "she sketches about as badly as any woman I ever saw, and *that's* saying a good deal. But she looks uncommonly well while she's at it. The fact is, Cummings," — Bartlett retires some feet from the canvas and squints at it, — "this very picture which you approve of so highly is — Miss Wyatt's. *I* couldn't attempt anything of the size of Ponkwasset! But she allows me to paint at it a little when she's away." Bartlett steals a look of joy at his friend's vexation, and then continues seriously : "I 've been having a curious time, Cummings." The other remains silent. "Don't you want to ask me about it ?"

Cummings: "I don't know that I do."

Bartlett : "Why, my dear old fellow, you' re hurt ! It *was* a silly joke, and I honestly ask your pardon." He lays down his brush and palette, and leaves the easel. "Cummings, I don't know what to do. I 'm in a perfect deuce of a state. I 'm hit — awfully hard ; and I don't know what to do about it. I wish I had gone at once — the first day. But I had to stay, — I had to stay." He turns and walks away from Cummings, whose eyes follow him in pardon and sympathy.

Cummings: " Do you really mean it, Bartlett ? I did n't dream of such a thing. I thought you were still brooding over that affair with Miss Harlan."

Bartlett : " Oh, child's play ! A prehistoric illusion ! A solar myth ! The thing never was." He rejects the obsolete superstition with a wave of his left hand. " I 'm in love with this girl, and I feel like a sneak and a brute about it. At the very

best it would be preposterous. Who am I, a poor
devil of a painter, the particular pet of Poverty, to
think of a young lady whose family and position
could command her the best? But putting that aside,
—putting that insuperable obstacle lightly aside, as
a mere trifle,—the thing remains an atrocity. It's
enormously indelicate to think of loving a woman
who would never have looked twice at me if I
had n't resembled an infernal scoundrel who tried
to break her heart; and I 've nothing else to com-
mend me. I 've the perfect certainty that she
does n't and can't care anything for me in myself;
and it grinds me into the dust to realize on what
terms she tolerates me. I could carry it off as a
joke, at first; but when it became serious, I had to
look it in the face; and that 's what it amounts to,
and if you know of any more hopeless and humili-
ating tangle, *I* don't." Bartlett, who has ap-
proached his friend during this speech, walks away
again; and there is an interval of silence.

Cummings, at last, musingly: "*You* in love with
Miss Wyatt? I can't imagine it!"

Bartlett, fiercely: "You can't imagine it? What's

the reason you can't imagine it? Don't be offensive, Cummings!" He stops in his walk and lowers upon his friend. "Why should n't I be in love with Miss Wyatt?"

Cummings: "Oh, nothing. Only you were saying"—

Bartlett: "I was saying! Don't tell me what *I* was saying. Say something yourself."

Cummings: "Really, Bartlett, you can't expect me to stand this sort of thing. You 're preposterous."

Bartlett: "I know it! But don't blame me. I beg your pardon. Is it because of the circumstances that you can't imagine my being in love with her?"

Cummings: "Oh, no; I was n't thinking of the circumstances; but it seemed so out of character for you"—

Bartlett, impatiently: "Oh, love 's always out of character, just as it 's always out of reason. I admit freely that I 'm an ass. And then?"

Cummings: "Well, then, I don't believe you have any more reason to be in despair than you have to be in love. If she tolerates you, as you say, it *can't* be because you look like the man who jilted her."

Bartlett : "Ah! But if she still loves *him?*"

Cummings : "You don't know that. That strikes me as a craze of jealousy. What makes you think she tolerates you for that reason or no-reason?"

Bartlett : "What makes me think it? From the very first she interpreted *me* by what she knew of *him.* She expected me to be this and not to be that; to have one habit and not another; and I could see that every time the fact was different, it was a miserable disappointment to her, a sort of shock. Every little difference between me and that other rascal gave her a start; and whenever I looked up I found her wistful eyes on me as if they were trying to puzzle me out; they used to follow me round the room like the eyes of a family portrait. You would n't have liked it yourself, Cummings. For the first three weeks I simply existed on false pretenses,—involuntary false pretenses, at that. I wanted to explode; I wanted to roar out, 'If you think I'm at all like that abandoned scoun-

drel of yours in anything but looks, I'm *not!*' But
I was bound by everything that was decent, to hold
my tongue, and let my soul be rasped out of me in
silence and apparent unconsciousness. That was
your fault. If you had n't told me all about the
thing I could have done something outrageous and
stopped it. But I was tied hand and foot by what
I knew. I had to let it go on."

Cummings: "I'm very sorry, Bartlett, but" —

Bartlett: "Oh, I dare say you would n't have
done it if you had n't had a wild ass of the desert
to deal with. Well, the old people got used to
some little individuality in me, by and by, and beyond a suppressed whoop or two from the mother
when I came suddenly into the room, they did n't
do anything to annoy me directly. But they were
anxious every minute for the effect on *her ;* and
it worried me as much to have *them* watching *her*
as to have *her* watching *me.* Of course I knew
that she talked this confounded resemblance over
with her mother every time I left them, and avoided
talking it over with the father."

Cummings: "But you say the trouble's over
now."

Bartlett: "Oh — *over!* No, it is n't over. When she's with me a while she comes to see that I am not a mere *doppelgänger.* She respites me to that extent. But I have still some small rags of self-esteem dangling about me; and now suppose I should presume to set up for somebody on my own account; the first hint of my caring for her as I do, if she could conceive of anything so atrocious, would tear open all the old sorrows. Ah! I can't think of it. Besides, I tell you, it is n't all over. It's only not so bad as it was. She's subject to relapses, when it's much worse than ever. Why" —Bartlett stands facing his friend, with a half-whimsical, half-desperate smile, as if about to illustrate his point, when Constance and her mother enter the parlor.

CONSTANCE, MRS. WYATT, BARTLETT, *and* CUM-
MINGS.

Constance, with a quick, violent arrest, "Ah!
Oh!"

Mrs. Wyatt: "Constance, Constance, darling!
What's the matter?"

Constance: "Oh, nothing — nothing." She
laughs, nervously. "I thought there was nobody
— here; and it — startled me. How do you do,
Mr. Cummings?" She goes quickly up to that
gentleman, and gives him her hand. "Don't you
think it wonderful to find such a day as this,
up here, at this time of year?" She struggles
to control the panting breath in which she speaks.

Cummings: "Yes, I supposed I had come quite
too late for anything of the sort. You must make
haste with your Ponkwasset, Miss Wyatt, or you'll
have to paint him with his winter cap on."

Constance: "Ah, yes! My picture. Mr. Bartlett has been telling you." Her eyes have already wandered away from Cummings, and they now dwell, with a furtive light of reparation and imploring upon Bartlett's disheartened patience: " Good *morning.*" It is a delicately tentative salutation, in a low voice, still fluttered by her nervous agitation.

Bartlett, in dull despair: " *Good* morning."

Constance: "How is the light on the mountain this morning?" She drifts deprecatingly up to the picture, near which Bartlett has stolidly kept his place.

Bartlett, in apathetic inattention: "Oh, very well, very well, indeed, thank you."

Constance, after a hesitating glance at him: " Did you like what I had done on it yesterday?"

Bartlett, very much as before: " Oh, yes; why not?"

Constance, with meek subtlety: " I was afraid I had vexed you — by it." She bends an appealing glance upon him, to which Bartlett remains impervious, and she drops her eyes with a faint sigh.

Then she lifts them again: "I was afraid I had — made the distance too blue."

Bartlett: "Oh, no; not at all."

Constance: "Do you think I had better try to finish it?"

Bartlett: "Oh, certainly. Why not? If it amuses you!"

Constance, perplexedly: "Of course." Then with a sad significance: "But I know I am trying your patience too far. You have been so kind, so good, I can't forgive myself for annoying you."

Bartlett: "It does n't annoy me. I'm very glad to be useful to you."

Constance, demurely: "I did n't mean painting; I meant — screaming." She lifts her eyes to Bartlett's face, with a pathetic, inquiring attempt at lightness, the slightest imaginable experimental archness in her self-reproach, which dies out as Bartlett frowns and bites the corner of his mustache in unresponsive silence. "I ought to be well enough now to stop it; I'm quite well enough to be ashamed of it." She breaks off a miserable little laugh.

Bartlett, with cold indifference: "There's no reason why you should stop it — if it amuses you." She looks at him in surprise at this rudeness. "Do you wish to try your hand at Ponkwasset this morning?"

Constance, with a flash of resentment: "No; thanks." Then with a lapse into her morbid self-abasement: "I shall not touch it again. Mamma!"

Mrs. Wyatt: "Yes, Constance." Mrs. Wyatt and Cummings, both intent on Bartlett and Constance, have been heroically feigning a polite interest in each other, from which pretense they now eagerly release themselves.

Constance: "Oh — nothing. I can get it of Mary. I won't trouble you." She goes toward the door.

Mrs. Wyatt: "Mary is n't up from her breakfast, yet. If you want anything, let me go with you, dear." She turns to follow Constance. "Good morning, Mr. Cummings; we shall see you at dinner. Good morning," — with an inquiring glance at Bartlett. Constance slightly inclines towards the two gentlemen without looking at them, in going out with her mother; and Cummings moves away to the piano, and affects to examine the sheet-music scattered over it.   Bartlett remains in his place near the easel.

III.

BARTLETT *and* CUMMINGS.

Bartlett, harshly, after a certain silence which his friend is apparently resolved not to break : "Sail in, Cummings!"

Cummings : "Oh, I've got nothing to say."

Bartlett : "Yes, you have. You think I'm a greater fool and a greater brute than you ever supposed in your most sanguine moments. Well, I am! What then ?"

Cummings, turning about from the music at which he has been pretending to look, and facing Bartlett, with a slight shrug : "If you choose to characterize your own behavior in that way, I shall not dispute you at any rate."

Bartlett : "Go on!"

Cummings : "Go on? You saw yourself, I suppose, how she hung upon every syllable you spoke, every look, every gesture ?"

Bartlett: " Yes, I saw it."

Cummings: " You saw how completely crushed she was by your tone and manner. You're not blind. Upon my word, Bartlett, if I did n't know what a good, kind-hearted fellow you are, I should say you were the greatest ruffian alive."

Bartlett, with a groan : " Go on ! That 's something like."

Cummings: " I could n't hear what was going on — I 'll own I tried — but I could see ; and to see the delicate *amende* she was trying to offer you, in such a way that it should not seem an amende, — a perfect study of a woman's gracious, unconscious art, — and then to see your sour refusal of it all, it made me sick."

Bartlett, with a desperate clutch at his face, like a man oppressed with some stifling vapor : " Yes, yes! I saw it all, too! And if it had been for *me,* I would have given anything for such happiness. Oh, gracious powers! How dear she is! I would rather have suffered any anguish than give her pain, and yet I gave her pain! I knew how it entered her heart : I felt it in my own. But

what could I do? If I am to be myself, if I am
not to steal the tenderness meant for another
man, the *love* she shows to me because I'm like
somebody else, I *must* play the brute. But have a
little mercy on me. At least, I'm a *baited* brute.
I don't know which way to turn, I don't know
what to do. She's so dear to me, — so dear in
every tone of her voice, every look of her eyes,
every aspiration or desire of her transparent soul,
that it seems to me my whole being is nothing but
a thought of her. I loved her helplessness, her
pallor, her sorrow; judge how I adore her return
to something like life! Oh, you blame me! You
simplify this infernal perplexity of mine and label
it brutality, and scold me for it. Great heaven!
And yet you saw, you heard how she entered this
room. In that instant the old illusion was back
on her, and *I* was nothing. All that I had been
striving and longing to be to her, and hoping and
despairing to seem, was swept out of existence; I
was reduced to a body without a soul, to a shadow,
a counterfeit! You think I resented it? Poor
girl, I *pitied* her so; and my own heart all the

time like lead in my breast, — a dull lump of ache!
I swear, I wonder I don't go mad. I suppose —
why, I suppose I *am* insane. No man in his senses
was ever bedeviled by such a maniacal hallucina-
tion. Look here, Cummings: tell me that this
damnable coil is n't simply a matter of my own
fancy. It 'll be some little relief to know that it 's
real.

Cummings: "It 's real enough, my dear fellow.
And it *is* a trial, — more than I could have believed such a fantastic thing could be."

Bartlett: "Trial? Ordeal by fire! Torment! I
can't stand it any longer."

Cummings, musingly: "She *is* beautiful, is n't
she, with that faint dawn of red in her cheeks, —
not a color, but a colored light like the light that
hangs round a rose-tree's boughs in the early
spring! And what a magnificent movement, what
a stately grace! The girl must have been a god-
dess!"

Bartlett: "And now she 's a saint — for sweet-
ness and patience! You think she 's had nothing
to suffer before from me? You know me better!
Well, I 'm going away."

Cummings: Perhaps it will be the best. You can go back with me to-morrow."

Bartlett: "To morrow? Go back with you to-morrow? What are you talking about, man?" Cummings smiles. "I can't go to-morrow. I can't leave her hating me."

Cummings: "I knew you never meant to go. Well, what will you do?"

Bartlett: "Don't be so cold-blooded! What would *you* do?"

Cummings: "I would have it out, somehow."

Bartlett: "Oh, you talk! How?"

Cummings: "I am not in love with Miss Wyatt."

Bartlett: "Oh, don't try to play the cynic with me! It does n't become you. I know I 've used you badly at times, Cummings. I behaved abominably in leaving you to take the brunt of meeting General Wyatt that first day; I said so then, and I shall always say it. But I thought you had forgiven that."

Cummings, with a laugh: "You make it hard to treat you seriously, Bartlett. What do you want me to do? Do you want me to go to Miss Wyatt, and explain your case to her?"

Bartlett, angrily: "No!"

Cummings: "Perhaps to Mrs. Wyatt?"

Bartlett, infuriate: "No!"

Cummings: "To the General?"

Bartlett, with sudden quiet: "You had better go away from here, Cummings — while you can."

Cummings: "I see you don't wish me to do anything, and you're quite right. Nobody *can* do anything but yourself."

Bartlett: "And what would you advise me to do?"

Cummings: "I've told you that I would have it out. You can't make matters worse. You can't go on in this way indefinitely. It's just possible that you might find yourself mistaken, — that Miss Wyatt cares for you in your own proper identity."

Bartlett: "For shame!"

Cummings: "Oh, if you like!"

Bartlett, after a pause: "Would you — would you see the General?"

Cummings: "If I wanted to marry the General.

Come, Bartlett; don't be ridiculous. You know you don't want my advice, and I have n't any to give. I must go to my room a moment."

Bartlett : "Well, go! You 're of no advantage here. You 'd have it out, would you? Well, then, I would n't. I 'm a brute, I know, and a fool, but I 'm not such a brute and fool as that!" Cummings listens with smiling patience, and then goes without reply, while Bartlett drops into the chair near the easel, and sulkily glares at the picture. Through the window at his back shows the mellow Indian summer landscape. The trees have all dropped their leaves, save the oaks which show their dark crimson banners among the deep green of the pines and hemlocks on the hills; the meadows, verdant as in June, slope away toward the fringe of birches and young maples along the borders of the pond; the low-blackberry trails like a running fire over the long grass limp from the first frosts, which have silenced all the insect voices. No sound of sylvan life is heard but the harsh challenge of a jay, answered from many trees of the nearest wood-lot. The far-off hill-tops are molten in the soft azure haze of the season; the nearer slopes and crests sleep under a grayer and thinner veil. It is to this scene that the painter turns from the easel, with the sullen unconsciousness in which he has dwelt upon the picture. Its beauty seems at last to penetrate his mood; he rises and looks upon it; then he goes out on the gallery, and, hidden by the fall of one of the curtains, stands leaning upon the rail and rapt in the common revery of the dreaming world. While he lingers there, Cummings appears at the door, and looks in; then with an air of some surprise, as if wondering not to see Bartlett, vanishes again, to give place to General Wyatt, who after a like research retires silently and apparently disconcerted. A few moments later Mrs. Wyatt comes to the threshold, and calling gently into the room, "Constance!" waits briefly and goes away. At last, the young girl herself appears, and falters in the doorway an instant, but finally comes forward and drifts softly and indirectly up to the picture, at which she glances with a little sigh. At the same moment Bartlett's voice, trolling a snatch of song, comes from the gallery without: —

ROMANCE.

I.

Here apart our paths, then, lie :
This way you wend, that way I ;
Speak one word before you go :
Do not, do not leave me so !

II.

What is it that I should say ?
Tell me quick ; I cannot stay ;
Quick ! I am not good at guessing :
Night is near, and time is pressing.

III.

Nay, then, go ! But were I you,
I will tell you what I'd do :
Rather than be baffled so,
I would never, never go ! ''

As the song ends, Bartlett reappears at the gallery door giving into the parlor, and encounters Constance turning at his tread from the picture on which she has been pensively gazing while he sang. He puts up a hand on either side of the door.

IV

BARTLETT *and* CONSTANCE.

Bartlett: "I did n't know you were here."

Constance: "Neither did I — know you were, till I heard you singing."

Bartlett, smiling ironically: "Oh, you did n't suppose I sang!"

Constance, confusedly: "I — I don't know" —

Bartlett: "Ah, you thought I did! I don't. I was indulging in a sort of modulated howling which I flatter myself is at least one peculiarity that's entirely my own. I was baying the landscape merely for my private amusement, and I'd not have done it, if I'd known you were in hearing. However, if it's helped to settle the fact one way or other, concerning any little idiosyncrasy of mine, I shan't regret it. I hope not to disappoint you in anything, by and by." He drops his hands from the doorposts and steps into the room, while Constance, in shrinking abeyance, stands trembling at his harshness.

Constance, in faltering reproach: "Mr. Bartlett!"

Bartlett: "Constance!"

Constance, struggling to assert herself, but breaking feebly in her attempt at hauteur: "Constance? What does this mean, Mr. Bartlett?"

Bartlett, with a sudden burst: "What does it mean? It means that I'm sick of this nightmare masquerade. It means that I want to be something to you — all the world to you — in and for myself. It means that I can't play another man's part any longer and live. It means that I love you, love you, love you, Constance!" He starts involuntarily toward her with outstretched arms, from which she recoils with a convulsive cry.

Constance: "You love me? *Me?* Oh, no, no! How can you be so merciless as to talk to me of love?" She drops her glowing face into her hands.

Bartlett: "Because I'm a man. Because love is more than mercy — better, higher, wiser. Listen to me, Constance! — yes, I will call you so now, if never again : you are so dear to me that I must say it at last if it killed you. If loving you is cruel, I'm pitiless! Give me some hope, tell me to breathe, my girl!"

Constance: "Oh go, while I can still forgive you."

Bartlett: " I won't go ; I won't have your forgiveness ; I will have all or nothing ; I want your love ! "

Constance, uncovering her face and turning its desolation upon him ; "My love? I have no love to give. My heart is dead."

Bartlett: "No, no ! That's part of the ugly trance that we've both been living in so long. Look ! You're better now than when you came here ; you're stronger, braver, more beautiful. My angel, you're turned a woman again ! Oh you can love me if you will ; and you will ! Look at me, darling !" He takes her listless right hand in his left, and gently draws her toward him.

Constance, starting away : "You're wrong ; you're all wrong ! You don't understand ; you don't know — Oh, listen to me !"

Bartlett, still holding her cold hand fast : " Yes, a thousand years. But you must tell me first that I may love you. That first ! "

Constance: " No ! That never ! And since you speak to me of love, listen to what it 's my right you should hear."

Bartlett, releasing her : " I don't care to hear. Nothing can ever change me. But if you bid me, I will go ! "

Constance : " You shall not go now till you know what despised and hated and forsaken thing you 've offered your love to."

Bartlett, beseechingly : " Constance, let me go while I can forgive myself. Nothing you can say will make me love you less ; remember that ; but I implore you to spare yourself. Don't speak, my love."

Constance: " Spare myself ? Not speak ? Not speak what has been on my tongue and heart and brain, a burning fire, so long ? — Oh, I was a happy girl once ! The days were not long enough for my happiness ; I woke at night to think of it. I was proud in my happiness and believed myself, poor fool, one to favor those I smiled on; and I had my vain and crazy dreams of being the happiness of some one who should come to ask for — what you ask now. Some one came. At first I didn't care for him, but he knew how to make me. He knew how to make my thoughts of him part of my happiness and pride and vanity till he was all in all, and I had no wish, no hope, no life but him; and then he — left me!" She buries her face in her hands again, and breaks into a low, piteous sobbing.

Bartlett, with a groan of helpless fury and compassion: "The fool, the sot, the slave! Constance, I knew all this, — I knew it from the first."

Constance, recoiling in wild reproach: "You *knew* it?"

Bartlett, desperately: "Yes, I knew it — in spite of myself, through my own stubborn fury I knew it, that first day, when I had obliged my friend to tell me what your father had told him, before I would hear reason. I would have given anything not to have known it then, when it was too late, for I had at least the grace to feel the wrong, the outrage of my knowing it. You can never pardon it, I see; but you must feel what a hateful burden I had to bear, when I found that I had somehow purloined the presence, the looks, the voice of another man — a man whom I would have joyfully changed myself to any monstrous shape *not* to resemble, though I knew that my likeness to him, bewildering you in a continual dream of him, was all that ever made you look at me or think of me. I lived in the hope — Heaven only knows why I should have had the hope! — that I might yet be myself to you; that you might wake from your dream of him and look on me in the daylight, and see that I was at least an honest man, and pity me and may be love me at last, as I loved you at first, from the moment I saw your dear, pale face, and heard your dear, sad voice." He follows up her slow retreat and again possesses himself of her hand: "Don't cast me off! It was monstrous, out of all decency, to know your sorrow; but I never tried to know it; I tried *not* to know it." He keeps fast hold of her hand, while she remains with averted head. "I love you,

Constance ; I loved you ; and when once you had bidden me stay, I was helpless to go away, or I would never be here now to offend you with the confession of that shameful knowledge. Do you think it was no trial to me? It gave me the conscience of an eavesdropper and a spy ; yet all I knew was sacred to me."

Constance, turning and looking steadfastly into his face : "And you could care for so poor a creature as I — so abject, so obtuse as never to know what had made her intolerable to the man that cast her off?"

Bartlett : "Man ? He was *no* man ! He" —

Constance, suddenly : "Oh, wait! I — I love him yet."

Bartlett, dropping her hand : " You " —

Constance : "Yes, yes ! As much as I live, I love him ! But when he left me, I seemed to die ; and now it's as if I were some wretched ghost clinging for all existence to the thought of my lost happiness. If that slips from me, then I cease to be."

Bartlett : "Why, this is still your dream. But

I won't despair. You'll wake yet, and care for me : I know you will."

Constance, tenderly : "Oh, I'm not dreaming now. I know that you are not he. You are everything that is kind and good ; and some day you will be very happy."

Bartlett, desolately : " I shall never be happy without your love." After a pause ; " It will be a barren, bitter comfort, but let me have it if you can : if *I* had met you first, could you have loved *me* ? "

Constance : " I might have loved you if — I had — lived." She turns from him again, and moves softly toward the door; his hollow voice arrests her.

Bartlett : " If you are dead, then I have lived too long. Your loss takes the smile out of life for me." A moment later : " You are cruel, Constance."

Constance, abruptly facing him : " I cruel ? To *you* ? "

Bartlett : " Yes, you have put me to shame before myself. You might have spared me ! A treacherous villain is false in time to save you from a life of betrayal, and you say your heart is dead. But that is n't enough. You tell me that you cannot care for me because you love that treacherous villain still. That's my disgrace, that's my humiliation, that's my killing shame. I could have borne all else. You might have cast me off however you would, driven me away with any scorn, whipped me from you with the sharpest rebuke that such presumption as mine could merit; but to drag a decent man's self-respect through such mire as that poor rascal's memory for six long weeks, and then tell him that you prefer the mire" —

Constance : "Oh, hush! I can't let you reproach him! He was pitilessly false to me, but I will be true to him forever. How do I know — I *must* find some reason for that, or there is no reason in anything! — how do I know that he did not break his word to me at my father's bidding? My father never liked him."

Bartlett, shaking his head with a melancholy smile: "Ah, Constance, do you think *I* would break my word to you at your father's bidding?"

Constance, in abject despair: "Well, then I go back to what I always knew; I was too slight, too foolish, too tiresome for his life-long love. He saw it in time, I don't blame him. You would see it, too."

Bartlett : "What devil's vantage enabled that infernal scoundrel to blight your spirit with his treason? Constance, is this my last answer ? "

Constance : "Yes, go! I am so sorry for you, —sorrier than I ever thought I could be for anything again."

Bartlett : "Then if you pity me, give me a little hope that sometime, somehow " —

Constance : "Oh, I have no hope, for you, for me, for any one. Good-by, good, kind friend! Try, —you won't have to try hard—to forget me. Unless some miracle should happen to show me that it was all his fault and none of mine, we are parting now forever. It has been a strange dream, and nothing is so strange as that it should be ending so. Are you the ghost or I, I wonder! It confuses me as it did at first; but if you are he, or only you— Ah, don't look at me so, or

I must believe he has never left me, and implore you to stay!"

Bartlett, quietly: "Thanks. I would not stay a moment longer in his disguise, if you begged me on your knees. I shall always love you, Constance, but if the world is wide enough, please Heaven, I will never see you again. There are some things dearer to me than your· presence. No, I won't take your hand; it can't heal the hurt your words have made, and nothing can help me, now I know from your own lips that but for my likeness to *him* I should never have been anything to you. Good-by!"

Constance: "Oh!" She sinks with a long cry into the arm-chair beside the table, and drops her head into her arms upon it. At the door toward which he turns Bartlett meets General Wyatt, and a moment later Mrs. Wyatt enters by the other. Bartlett recoils under the concentrated reproach and inquiry of their gaze.

V.

General Wyatt, Mrs. Wyatt, Constance, *and* Bartlett.

Mrs. Wyatt, hastening to bow herself over Constance's fallen head: "Oh, what is it, Constance?" As Constance makes no reply, she lifts her eyes again to Bartlett's face.

General Wyatt, peremptorily: "Well, sir!"

Bartlett, with bitter desperation: "Oh, you shall know!"

Constance, interposing: "I will tell! You shall be spared that, at least." She has risen, and with her face still hidden in her handkerchief, seeks her father with an outstretched hand. He tenderly gathers her to his arms, and she droops a moment upon his shoulder; then, with an electrical revolt against her own weakness, she lifts her head and dries her tears with a passionate energy. "He — Oh, speak *for* me!" Her head falls again on her father's shoulder.

Bartlett, with grave irony and self-scorn: "It's a simple matter, sir; I have been telling Miss Wyatt that I love her, and offering to share with her my obscurity and poverty. I"—

General Wyatt, impatiently: "Curse your poverty, sir! I'm poor myself. Well!"

Bartlett: "Oh, that's merely the beginning; I have had the indecency to do this, knowing that what alone rendered me sufferable to her it was a cruel shame for me to know, and an atrocity for me to presume upon. I"—

General Wyatt: "I authorized this knowledge on your part when I spoke to your friend, and before he went away he told me all he had said to you."

Bartlett, in the first stages of petrifaction: "Cummings?"

General Wyatt: "Yes."

Bartlett: "Told you that I knew whom I was like?"

General Wyatt: "Yes."

Bartlett, very gently: "Then I think that man will be lost for keeping his conscience *too* clean. Cummings has invented a new sin."

Mrs. Wyatt: "James, James! You told me that Mr. Bartlett did n't know."

General Wyatt, contritely: "I let you think so, Margaret; I did n't know what else to do."

Mrs. Wyatt: "Oh, James!"

Constance: "Oh, papa!" She turns with bowed head from her father's arms, and takes refuge in her mother's embrace. General Wyatt, released, fetches a compass round about the parlor, with a face of intense dismay. He pauses in front of his wife.

General Wyatt: "Margaret, you must know the worst, now."

Mrs. Wyatt, in gentle reproach, while she softly caresses Constance's hair: "Oh, is there anything *worse*, James?"

General Wyatt, hopelessly: "Yes: I'm afraid I have been to blame,"

Bartlett: "General Wyatt, let me retire. I"—

General Wyatt: "No, sir. This concerns you,

10

too, now. Your destiny has entangled you with our sad fortunes, and now you must know them all."

Constance, from her mother's shoulder: "Yes, stay, — whatever it is. If you care for me, nothing can hurt you any more, now."

General Wyatt: "Margaret, — Constance! If I have been mistaken in what I have done, you must try somehow to forgive me; it was my tenderness for you both misled me, if I erred. Sir, let me address my defense to you. You can see the whole matter with clearer eyes than we." At an imploring gesture from Bartlett, he turns again to Mrs. Wyatt. "Perhaps you are right, sir. Margaret, when I had made up my mind that the wretch who had stolen our child's heart was utterly unfit and unworthy " —

Constance, starting away from her mother with a cry: "Ah, you *did* drive him from me, then! I knew, I knew it! And after all these days and weeks and months that seem years and centuries of agony, you tell me that it was *you* broke my heart! No, no, I never *will* forgive you, father! Where is he? Tell me that! Where is my husband — the husband you robbed me of? Did you kill him, when you chose to crush my life? Is he dead? If he's living I will find him wherever he is. No distance and no danger shall keep me from him. I'll find him and fall down before him, and implore *him* to forgive you, for I never can! Was this your tenderness for me — to drive him away, and leave me to the pitiless humiliation of believing myself deserted? Oh, great tenderness!"

General Wyatt, confronting her storm with perfect quiet: "No, I will give better proof of my tenderness than that." He takes from his pocket-book a folded paper which he hands to his wife: "Margaret, do you know that writing?"

Mrs. Wyatt, glancing at the superscription: "Oh, too well! This is to you, James."

General Wyatt : "It's for you, now. Read it."

Mrs. Wyatt, wonderingly unfolding the paper and then reading: "'*I confess myself guilty of forging Major Cummings's signature, and in consideration of his and your own forbearance, I promise never to see Miss Wyatt again. I shall always be grateful for your mercy; and'*— James, James! It is n't possible!"

Constance, who has crept nearer and nearer while her mother has been reading, as if drawn by a resistless fascination: "No, it is n't possible! It's false; it's a fraud! I *will* see it." She swiftly possesses herself of the paper and scans the handwriting for a moment with a fierce intentness. Then she flings it wildly away. "Yes, yes, it's true! It's his hand. It's true, it's the only true thing in this world of lies!" She totters away toward the sofa. Bartlett makes a movement to support her, but she repulses him, and throws herself upon the cushions.

General Wyatt: "Sir, I am sorry to make you the victim of a scene. It has been your fate, and no part of my intention. Will you look at this paper? You don't know all that is in it yet." He touches it with his foot.

Bartlett, in dull dejection: "No, I won't look at it. If it were a radiant message from heaven, I don't see how it could help me now."

Mrs. Wyatt: "I'm afraid you've made a terrible mistake, James."

General Wyatt: "Margaret! Don't say that!"

Mrs. Wyatt: "Yes, it would have been better to show us this paper at once, — better than to keep us all these days in this terrible suffering."

General Wyatt: " I was afraid of greater suffering for you both. I chose sorrow for Constance rather than the ignominy of knowing that she had set her heart on so base a scoundrel. When he crawled in the dust there before me, and whined for pity, I revolted from telling you or her how vile he was; the thought of it seemed to dishonor you; and I had hoped something, everything, from my girl's self-respect, her obedience, her faith in me. I never dreamed that it must come to this."

Mrs. Wyatt, sadly shaking her head: "I know how well you meant; but oh, it was a fatal mistake!"

Constance, abandoning her refuge among the cushions, and coming forward to her father: " No, mother, it was no mistake! I see now how wise and kind and merciful you have been, papa. You can never love me again, I've behaved so badly; but if you'll let me, I will try to live my gratitude for your mercy at a time when the whole truth would have killed me. Oh, papa! What shall I say, what shall I do to show how sorry and ashamed I am? Let me go down on my knees to thank you." Her father catches her to his heart, and fondly kisses her again and again. "I don't deserve it, papa! You ought to hate me, and drive me from you, and never let me see you again." She starts away from him as if to execute upon herself this terrible doom, when her eye falls upon the letter where she had thrown it on the floor. "To think how long I have been the fool, the slave of that — *felon!*" She stoops upon the paper with a hawk-like fierceness; she tears it into shreds, and strews the fragments about the room. "Oh, if I could only tear out of my heart all thoughts of him, all memory, all likeness!" In her wild scorn she has whirled unheedingly away toward Bartlett, whom, suddenly confronting, she apparently addresses in this aspiration; he opens wide his folded arms.

Bartlett: "And what would you do, then, with this extraordinary resemblance?" The closing circle of his arms involves her and clasps her to his heart, from which beneficent shelter she presently exiles herself a pace or two and stands with either hand pressed against his breast while her eyes dwell with rapture on his face.

Constance: "Oh, *you're* not like him, and you *never* were!"

Bartlett, with light irony: "Ah?"

Constance: "If I had not been blind, blind, blind, I never could have seen the slightest similarity. Like *him?* Never!"

Bartlett: "Ah! Then perhaps the resemblance, which we have noticed from time to time, and which has been the cause of some annoyance and embarrassment all round, was simply a disguise which I had assumed for the time being to accomplish a purpose of my own?"

Constance: "Oh, don't jest it away! It's your soul that I see now, your true and brave and generous heart; and if you pardoned me for mistaking you a single moment for one who had neither soul nor heart, I could never look you in the face again!"

Bartlett : " You seem to be taking a good provisional glare at me beforehand, then, Miss Wyatt. I've never been so nearly looked out of countenance in my life. But you need n't be afraid ; I shall not pardon your crime."   Constance abruptly drops her head upon his breast, and again instantly repels herself.

Constance : " No, you must not if you could. But.you can't — you can't care for me after hearing what I could say to my father " —

Bartlett : " That was in a moment of great excitement."

Constance : " After hearing me rave about a man so unworthy of — any one — you cared for No, your self-respect — everything — demands that you should cast me off."

Bartlett : " It does. But I am inexorable, — you must have observed the trait before. In this case I will not yield even to my own colossal self-respect."   Earnestly: " Ah, Constance, do you think I could love you the less because your heart was too true to swerve even from a traitor till he was proved as false to honor as to you ? "   Lightly again: " Come, I like your fidelity to worthless people; I'm rather a deep and darkling villain myself."

Constance, devoutly : " You ? Oh, you are as nobly frank and open as — as — as papa ! "

Bartlett : " No, Constance, you are wrong, for once. Hear my dreadful secret: I'm not what I seem, — the light and joyous creature I look, — I'm an emotional wreck. Three short years ago, I was frightfully jilted "— they all turn upon him in surprise — " by a young person who, I'm sorry to say, has n't yet consoled me by turning out a scamp."

Constance, drifting to his side with a radiant smile: " Oh, I'm *so* glad."

Bartlett, with affected dryness: " Are you ? I did n't know it was such a laughing matter. I was always disposed to take those things seriously."

Constance : " Yes, yes ! But don't you see ? It places us on more of an equality." She looks at him with a smile of rapture and logic exquisitely compact.

Bartlett: "Does it? But you're not half as happy as I am."

Constance: "Oh, yes, I am! Twice."

Bartlett: "Then that makes us just even, for so am I." They stand ridiculously blest, holding each other's hand a moment, and then Constance, still clinging to one of his hands, goes and rests her other arm upon her mother's shoulder.

Constance: "Mamma, how wretched I have made you, all these months!"

Mrs. Wyatt: "If your trouble's over now, my child,"—she tenderly kisses her cheek,—"there's no trouble for your mother in the world."

Constance: "But I'm not happy, mamma. I can't be happy, thinking how wickedly unhappy I've been. No, no! I had better go back to the old wretched state again; it's all I'm fit for. I'm *so* ashamed of myself. Send him away!" She renews her hold upon his hand.

Bartlett: "Nothing of the kind. I was requested to remain here six weeks ago, by a young lady. Besides, this is a public house. Come, I haven't finished the catalogue of my disagreeable qualities

yet. I'm jealous. I want you to put that arm
on *my* shoulder." He gently effects the desired
transfer, and then, chancing to look up, he discov-
ers the Rev. Arthur Cummings on the threshold
in the act of modestly retreating. He detains him
with a great melodramatic start. "Hah! A clergyman! This is indeed ominous!"